MW01616267

THE HEBREW SCRIPTURES
[SO-CALLED *"OLD TESTAMENT"*]

AND

THE GREEK SCRIPTURES:
[SO-CALLED *"NEW TESTAMENT"*]

The Vast Differences, Similarities, Glories and Contradictions

Δ

By

MOSES FARRAR

Biblical Historian and Researcher

MONÄMI PUBLICATIONS
PHILADELPHIA, PENNSYLVANIA

Copyright © 2007 by Moses Farrar

First Printing: March 2007

Printed in the United States of America

TABLE OF CONTENTS

Preface ....vii-x

I A FEW PRELIMINARY FACTS ON THE TOPIC 11

II THE GLORY & BEAUTY OF THE HEBREW SCRIPTURES 13

III THE GREEK SCRIPTURES (N.T.): SIMILARITIES &
DISSIMILARITIES TO THE HEBREW SCRIPTURES (O.T.) ... 37

IV DID YESHUA (Jesus) REALLY SAY THAT? 43

V HOW CHRISTIANITY 'STOLE' JESUS & ADOPTED
HIM AS ITS FOUNDER & SAVIOUR-GOD 59

VI THE BEST OF THE GREEK SCRIPTURES (N.T.) 69

VII IF YESHUA (Jesus) WAS NOT/IS NOT THE SAVIOUR
OF THE WORLD, WHO, THEN, IS? 81

VIII IS CHRIST 'OUR PASSOVER', AS PAUL CLAIMS? 88

IX WHY THE TERM 'SO-CALLED' IN REFERENCE TO
OLD TESTAMENT & NEW TESTAMENT? 98

X CRUCIFIXION, RESURRECTION, ASCENSION,
ALIVE FOR EVER? 104

XI **O! TO BE BLACK!** *(A Must-Read Chapter)* **114**

XII THE HEBREW ALPHABET & A FEW EVERYDAY
PHRASES 125

ABOUT THE AUTHOR 129

BOOKS' ORDER FORMS 130-131

iii

DEDICATIONS

To My Beloved Mother
the Late SAINT LAVINIA FARRAR
(pious, refined, intelligent)

To FOUR GREAT RABBIS
(three deceased, one yet lives)

To the Late
ELDER EDWARD and SAINT BERTHA SUYDAM
My childhood mentors in the Printing Trade

Israel's Watchword and Confession of Faith:

שְׁמַע יִשְׂרָאֵל, יְיָ אֱלֹהֵינוּ, יְיָ ׀ אֶחָד:

Sh'ma, Yisrael: Adonai Elohénu Adonai Echod.

"Hear, O Israel: THE LORD IS OUR GOD, THE LORD IS ONE."

(Deuteronomy 6:4, H.S.)

THE MAIN PURPOSE OF THIS BOOK:

"To proclaim the name of
YAHWEH (the LORD),
and to ascribe greatness unto
Elohim (God)."

FOREWORD

I GIVE ALL WORSHIP, PRAISE AND GLORY TO יהוה (YAH – the LORD), *the Almighty and Most High Elohim* (God): *the Elohim of Abraham, the Elohim of Isaac, and the Elohim of Jacob.* "*This* [YAH] *is My name for ever, and this* [YAH] *is My memorial unto all generations.*"

(Exodus 3:15, HEBREW HOLY SCRIPTURES, Masoretic Text)

THE BOOK KNOWN AS THE BIBLE is the world's best-seller, and has been for hundreds of years, even thousands. Versions of the Bible, or at least of parts of it, are now found in almost every language spoken on the globe. Yet, the word *Bible* does not appear anywhere within its text. Also absent from the text of the Bible are the terms *Old Testament* and *New Testament.* The latter term, however, needs to be qualified: The words *new testament* do appear, uncapitalized, in the Gospels of Matthew, Mark, and Luke, but are in no way referring to the compilation of those books from Matthew to Revelation, designated as "The New Testament."

In this book, my sixth, I will address the three questions on the front cover, as well as scores of other subjects in both the Hebrew Scriptures (so-called Old Testament) and the Greek Scriptures (so-called New Testament). There are major and critical differences between these two volumes which heretofore have seldom been explored, many of which have risen to the level of conflict. Those places in Matthew, Mark, and Luke, mentioned in the paragraph above, will be discussed under the chapter heading, "DID YESHUA [JESUS] REALLY SAY THAT?"

Since the two Testaments are poles apart on so many of their themes, I question whether they should even be

vii

under the same cover. The sacred scriptures of other religions, e.g., Islam, Buddhism, Hinduism, and Zorastrianism, do not have attached to them the writings of another persuasion. And if there were such an attachment, there would certainly be a harmonious balance between the first and second portions, and not more than half of the latter section abrogating the former.

So many versions of the Bible and so many different interpretations are responsible for millions of people being confused to the point where they no longer know what to believe. To those in such a state, we admonish you to allow this Scriptural passage, which is one among hundreds, to serve as your guide:

"To the law and to the testimony: if they speak not according to this word, it is because there is no light in them" (Isaiah 8:20).

"The law" and "the testimony" referred to in the above scripture are The Ten Commandments. I will expound further on this topic in the pages that follow.

The ultimate purpose of this book is to exalt the Most High and Almighty Creator, and to proclaim His Holy Law and the teaching of His prophets. I realize that there are forces at work, which cease not day nor night, striving to destroy the holy and righteous way established by Moses and the prophets, through the power of the Supreme Being. In this book I will strongly oppose those evil forces with all that is within me. I say in concert with the Psalmist,

"Let God arise, and let His enemies be scattered . . ."

Our mission on the earth as Hebrew Israelites is proclaimed, in part, by the Most High through the prophet Isaiah (42:6-7):

"I the LORD have called thee in righteousness, and will

viii

hold thine hand, and will keep thee, and give thee for
a covenant of the people, for a light of the Gentiles;
<u>⁷To open the blind eyes, to bring out the prisoners</u>
<u>from the prison, and them that sit in darkness out of</u>
<u>the prison house.</u>"

Slavery and the slavemaster's religion have spiritually blinded the eyes and imprisoned and sentenced thousands of people of African ancestry to utter darkness in the prison house. But there's a quiet storm rising among Black people in the Western Hemisphere and in parts of Black Africa, as well, as many awaken to reclaim the knowledge and will of their True Creator. In my brief career as an author (now in my eleventh year), hundreds of letters and telephone calls have been received by me from many living in the Virgin Islands, Canada, the countries of South Africa, Zimbabwe, Malawi, the Caribbean, and, of course, from several areas of the United States. They are all welcoming and embracing another point of view from reading the works of such celebrated authors as Rudolph Windsor, Joseph Williams, Steven Jacobs, Ella Hughley, Cohane Michael ben Levy, and *Yours Truly.* A Hebrew Israelite newspaper out of Memphis, Tennessee, *The Jerusalem Chronicle,* published by Bro. Yehoshaphat ben Israel, is also playing a major role in enlightening the people who for more than 400 years have sat in spiritual solitary confinement.

As I have learned, so will I impart. This book will differ in many ways from my previous ones, in that it will even offer, among other things, an opportunity for the reader to familiarize him- or herself with the Hebrew alphabet and a few important self-pronouncing Hebrew words and phrases.

As in my previous publications, I strongly suggest that

ix

you not only read this book, but that you rigorously and energetically study it!

Although some portions of this book may be rather stinging at times, as neglected essential truths often are, please bear in mind that the object of this message is not to offend, but to enlighten, and to awaken the reader to the urgency of the times. The Holy One of Israel is commanding His people to "come out of Babylon, and be not partakers of her sins, nor receive her plagues." The times are evil, the world is wicked, and there are wars and rumors of wars – all because mankind, for the most part, has not sought its Maker, the Creator of the universe.

The message of the prophet Hosea of nearly 2,800 years ago still rings true today:

> *"My people are destroyed for lack of knowledge: because thou hast rejected knowledge, I will also reject thee, that thou shalt be no priest to Me: seeing thou hast forgotten the law of thy God, I will also forget thy children"* (Hosea 4:6).

If we would but unify under the banner of the Most High God's Holy Law, the prophecy of Hosea would then be reversed, and we would be found under the more glorious prophecy of Isaiah (45:17):

> *"But Israel shall be saved in the LORD with an everlasting salvation: ye shall not be ashamed nor confounded world without end."*

Surely that day approaches, for He who has promised is faithful. The Almighty God, and He alone, is your Savior and your King. Trust Him, keep His Holy Law, and He shall bring it to pass.

CHAPTER 1

A Few Preliminary Facts On the Topic

MOST VERSIONS OF THE BIBLE contain 66 books; 39 of them (59.1%) comprise what common era historians have designated as "The Old Testament." Likewise, the so-called "New Testament" is comprised of 27 books (40.9%). The exception to the above are the *Hebrew versions, many of which have been translated into English, none of which have a New Testament, and all are made up of books from Genesis to Malachi.

In the Old Testament, the Almighty and Most High God is the Central Being. The Creator is referred to as early as the fourth word of the text: *"In the beginning †Elohim [God] created the heaven and the earth"* (Gen. 1:1), and 24 additional times in the first chapter of Genesis. In the New Testament, Jesus is the central figure. The word *Lord,* referring to the Most High God, does not appear until Matthew 1:20, and that is in reference to the birth of Jesus, where *"the angel of the* Lord *appeared unto him* [Joseph] *in a dream . . ."*

In Genesis 2, which contains 25 verses, the phrases LORD and LORD God appear 13 times, and in addition, nine pronouns for God are used (He, His, and I). Out of the 23 verses in Matthew 2, *Lord* and *God* occur a total of just four times.

---

*We recommend the Hebrew version (English translation) under the title *The Holy Scriptures, According to the Masoretic Text.*

†Some Hebrew versions (English translation) carry *Elohim* throughout their texts, instead of "God." Another version uses *Hashem* (The Name). The Masoretic carries "God" and "LORD" entirely.

The greater portion of any body of sacred writings should exalt, extol, hallow, magnify and praise the object of its worship. This the Old Testament scriptures do in each of its 39 books, with the exception of the Books of Esther and the Song of Solomon, in which no references to God are found. We find that the Almighty and Most High God is at the very center of almost the entire Old Testament narratives. Although the writings in many instances focus on the lives and works of Abraham, Moses and the children of Israel, Isaiah, Jeremiah, David, Solomon, etc., etc., the messages therein are always theocentric. This is not true for the most part with the New Testament, for the creature (Jesus) is exalted and oftentimes even worshipped moreso than the Creator. However, Jesus is not responsible for this, but many of those who came after him have forced this idolatrous practice upon the world.

Before we proceed further, let us introduce a list of new terminologies that will be used throughout the rest of this book:
The term *Hebrew Scriptures,* and in a few instances the Hebrew term *Tanakh* (pronounced Ta-NÖK), will be used instead of *Old Testament.* (The letters *O.T.* may sometimes appear in parentheses for clarity.) The term *New Testament* will be replaced by *Greek Scriptures;* these are really their proper designations. The first five books of the Hebrew Scriptures (Genesis through Deuteronomy) are called *Torah,* which means "teaching" and/or "law"; but in their entirety, the books from Genesis to Malachi are called the *Hebrew Scriptures,* or the *Tanakh.*

In addition, hereafter when referring to Jesus, we will employ the use of his Hebrew name, *Yeshua ben Yosef* (or just *Yeshua*), which translates into English as "Joshua son of Joseph." "Jesus" may appear in parentheses at times. (Yeshua is pronounced Yĕ-SHŪ-a.) The Latin *Iésous Christos* became *Jesus Christ.*

CHAPTER 2

The Glory & Beauty of The Hebrew Scriptures

WE HAVE ALREADY ADDRESSED how that the Eternal One, King of the universe (often referred to in the English-speaking world as *God,* the LORD *God,* and in other expressions of majesty) is prominently placed at the very top of the two opening chapters of the Hebrew Scriptures. As we progress further into the Book of Genesis, we find this same compassionate God giving mankind a chance to repent and be saved from destruction when He commands the prophet Noah to herald His message of salvation to the people of his day and to build an ark of gopher wood. There is a glorious passage of scripture from the Noachal period, found in Gen. 6:8-9:

> *"But Noah found grace in the eyes of the LORD. . . . Noah was a just man and *perfect in his generations, and Noah walked with God."*

Ten generations later Abram is called by the Almighty and is commanded to leave the city of Ur in the country of Chaldea, the land of his nativity where he had engaged in idolatry from his birth, and directs him to go to the land of Canaan, with his wife, servants and substance (Gen. 12:1-5). Now both the Chaldeans (Babylonians) and the Canaanites were of the Black race, as was Abram. (Let us not now dwell on this point, however; its significance will appear later on in the book.)

Abram, at age 99, was told by God to *"walk before Me, and be thou *perfect,"* and He changed his name from Abram

---

*The word *perfect* in biblical language means *upright, sincere.*

to Abra<u>ham</u>. The Most High proclaimed him as the father of a multitude of nations; all the biblical prophets, priests, kings and common people of Hebrew-Israelite ancestry were of the seed of Abraham. His obedience to and faith in the Almighty, and his willingness to forsake his idolatrous ways gained him a place in the annals of Scripture and biblical history as the only being whom the Eternal One called, *"God's friend forever."*

All told, the various forms of his name (Abram, Abraham, Abram's, Abraham's) appears 220 times in the Hebrew Scriptures, and 74 times in the Greek Scriptures.

"The LORD, God Most High, Maker of heaven and earth," as Abraham once proclaimed Him (Gen. 14:22), spoke many wondrous words about this righteous patriarch, among them this affirmation, which is one of the cherished passages in Torah:

> *"For I know him, that he will command his children and his household after him, and they shall keep the way of the LORD, to do justice and judgment, that the LORD may bring upon Abraham that which He hath spoken of him"* (Gen. 18:19).

Certainly there are several other great personalities recorded within the Book of Genesis of whom the Almighty Himself has grandly spoken and who themselves have left on record words of exaltation of their Maker. There were Isaac and Jacob, to whom the Most High made the exact same promise that He made to Abraham: *". . . And in thee shall all families and nations of the earth be blessed."* Also, there were Joseph, Sarah, Rebecca, Rachel and Leah, patriarch and matriarchs of the Hebrew-Israelite people, who placed the Great I AM at the very center of their existence.

As we continue with the ***Glory and Beauty of the Hebrew Scriptures*** and direct the attention of the reader to men and women of God to whom He revealed Himself in a mighty and awe-inspiring way, certainly **Moses, L**awgiver and father of the prophets, stands head and shoulders above the rest, spiritually speaking.

The books Exodus through Deuteronomy are replete with Moses' greatness, but his life's song doesn't end with the close of the Torah. The name *Moses* (in Hebrew, Mō-SHÉ) appears 730 times in the Hebrew Scriptures (O.T.) and 80 times in the Greek Scriptures (N.T.). All those who succeeded him, from Joshua to Malachi to Yeshua, held Moses in very high regard. It is necessary to note here that Yeshua never said that he was "more worthy than Moses"; Paul, in error, made that claim.

Assuming that the reader is already familiar with the life of Moses, we will not spend time retelling it. However, the question does often arise, "Was Moses the greatest of all the prophets?" In most Israelite circles Moses is considered to be a cut above the other prophets, and in Hebraic commentary is called "the father of the prophets."

In the episode where Moses' brother and sister, Aaron and Miriam, spoke against him because he married a Cushite (Ethiopian) woman (Numbers 12:6-8, H.S.), the Almighty strongly implies that Moses was a cut above the prophets who were to succeed him:

> *⁶And He said: 'Hear now My words: if there be a prophet among you, I the LORD do make Myself known unto him in a vision, I do speak with him in a dream. ⁷My servant Moses is not so; he is trusted in all My house; with him do I speak mouth to mouth, even manifestly, and not in dark speeches; and the similitude of the LORD doth he behold; wherefore then were ye not afraid to speak against my servant, against Moses?'*

From the verses above, particularly the underscored portions, it seems clear that the Most High and Moses had a relationship with each other that was different than with the prophets succeeding him. After the vision of the burning bush, Moses experienced no further dreams or visions from God, but talked with Him "mouth to mouth"; but to his successors He always appeared through the medium of dreams and visions (vs. 6), as evidenced by the testimonies of most of the other biblical prophets. Hosea 12:13 may be the only scripture where it is stated that Moses was a prophet, although he is not named.

In Yeshua's (Jesus') **parable** of the *Rich Man and Lazarus* (Luke 16:19-31), he distinguishes Moses. The story states, in brief, that the Rich Man lifts up his eyes in hell and cries to father Abraham, who has received Lazarus into his bosom, to release Lazarus that he may go and tell his five brothers to repent so that they will not end up in hell.

Father Abraham speaks very kindly to the Rich Man, even calls him "son." But in the final analysis Abraham makes reference, not once but twice, to *Moses and the prophets,* saying to the Rich Man concerning his five brothers (in Luke 16:29):

> *"They have Moses and the prophets; let them hear them." And he said, "Nay, father Abraham,: but if one went unto them from the dead, they will repent." And he said unto him, "If they hear not Moses and the prophets, neither will they be persuaded, though one rose from the dead."*

If we are to answer the question, *"Was Moses the greatest of all the prophets?,"* we would first have to group him with the prophets, for the sake of convenience. And if we do that, then the answer to the question would be "Yes," but with reservation. When we consider all the great work which Moses did: Going before Pharoah, bringing about the plagues, leading Israel out of Egypt and organizing them into a nation, and teaching them commandments, statutes and judgments, then, yes, he was the greatest prophet. But on the other hand, for example, if God commands another prophet just to turn over a stone, and he does that with all his heart, soul and might, then he is just as great, because he has obeyed the voice of the Almighty. From this viewpoint, then, one prophet is no greater than the other.

As we examine Deuteronomy 34:10-12, let us bear in mind that the passage speaks in terms of the volume and magnitude of work performed by Moses, as stated above:

[10] *"And there arose not a prophet since in Israel like unto Moses, whom the* LORD *knew face to face,* [11]*In all the signs and the wonders, which the* LORD *sent him to do in the land of Egypt to Pharoah, and to all his servants, and to all his land,* [12]*And in all that mighty hand, and in all the great terror which Moses showed in the sight of all Israel."*

There are several other majestic scriptures which declare how Moses found favor with the Almighty and stood in awe of His mighty and limitless power.

As we continue to show the *Glory and Beauty of the Hebrew Scriptures,* there are two more examples of Moses' relationship with the Most High which we believe to be of special interest, before moving on to discuss the Divine encounters of other stalwart men and women of biblical times.

The first event tells of Moses' refusal to go any further in leading the children of Israel through the wilderness unless he has the blessed assurance that God's presence will go with them. The burden of leadership and the journey through the wilderness with such a great multitude has taken its toll on Moses, to the point that he has become weary. Despite all the problems facing him, he is still willing to travel on toward the banks of the River Jordan, but only if armed with the promise from the Most High Himself that he and the Israelites would not be left to bear the burden alone.

In Exodus 33:12-16 you can almost hear the frustration in Moses' voice as he pleads with the Almighty:

[12]*And Moses said unto the* LORD, *'See, Thou sayest unto me: Bring up this people; and Thou hast not let me know whom Thou wilt send with me. Yet Thou hast said: I know thee by name, and thou hast also found grace in My sight.* [13]*Now therefore, I pray Thee, if I have found grace in Thy sight, show me now Thy ways, that I may know Thee, to the end that I may find grace in Thy sight; and consider that this nation is Thy people.'* [14]*And He said: 'My presence shall go with thee, and I will give thee rest.'* [15]*And he said unto Him: 'If Thy presence go not with me, carry us not up hence.* [16]*For wherein now shall*

it be known that I have found grace in Thy sight, I and Thy people? is it not in that Thou goest with us, so that we are distinguished, I and Thy people, from all the people that are upon the face of the earth?'

In this, our final episode on Moses, we find him pleading with the Almighty and Most High God, requesting to be shown His glory. His plea begins in Exodus 33:18, 19, and its fulfillment in Exodus 34:6-8:

> [18]*And he said: 'Show me, I pray Thee, Thy glory.'* [19]*And He said: 'I will make all My goodness pass before thee, and will proclaim the name of the LORD before thee . . .'*

Even though the Most High promised to allow Moses to behold His glory, He cautioned him that neither he nor any other being *"can see My 'face,' for no man can see Me and live."* (The commentary on this passage is forthcoming.) So, in 33:20-23, the Almighty takes Moses where probably no one else before or since has gone – to the pinnacle of spirituality, without actually piercing the very veil of His Divine Essence, saying unto him:

> [20]*"Thou canst not see My face, for man shall not see Me and live.'* [21]*And the LORD said: 'Behold, there is a place by Me, and thou shalt stand upon the rock.* [22]*And it shall come to pass, while My glory passeth by, that I will put thee in a cleft of the rock, and will cover thee with My hand until I have passed by.* [23]*And I will take away My hand, and thou shalt see My back; but My face shall not be seen.'*

And, finally, in 34:6-8, the Most High delivers on His promise, showing Moses His glory:

> [6]*And the LORD passed by before him, and proclaimed: 'The LORD, the LORD, God, merciful and gracious, long-suffering and abundant in goodness and truth;* [7]*keeping mercy unto the thousandth generation, forgiving iniquity and transgression and sin, and that will by no means clear the guilty; visiting the iniquity of the fathers upon the children, and upon the children's children, unto the third and fourth generation.'* [8]*And Moses made haste, and bowed his head and worshipped.*

From the Foremost Commentary: Ex. 33:18,19,20,23

In verse 18, the phrase *show me Thy glory:* Emboldened by the success of his plea on behalf of the people, Moses begs the privilege of being acquainted with 'the glory of God', i.e. with His eternal qualities.

In verse 19, the phrase *My goodness:* God's moral attributes. The revelation of these Attributes of love and mercy is the source of the sublime principle of the *Imitation of God.* Israel is not only to serve God, but to imitate Him. Mortal man, however, cannot imitate God's infinity, omnipotence or eternity. That side of His nature, which is beyond human comprehension, is also beyond human imitation. But we can know His 'goodness', and we can follow *His ways of mercy and forgiveness.* Thus, pity is a Divine attribute; and man is never nearer to the Divine than in his compassionate moments. God's merciful qualities are, therefore, the most real links between God and Man. 'Even as I am merciful, be thou merciful; even as I am gracious, be thou gracious,' is the Hebrew-Israelite translation of the great commandment of the Imitation of God.

In verse 20, the phrase *see My face:* Moses desires to know what no human being can fathom, what no human language can express. His request, however, is not due to curiosity, but in order to confirm the promise of the Almighty in verse 14, *'My presence shall go with thee, and I will give thee rest.'*

In verse 23, the phrase *My face shall not be seen:* When God passes by, presumably in the form of fire (see Ex. 24:17), Moses will be sheltered in 'a cleft of the rock'. He will thus not see 'the face', the full Manifestation of the Divine radiance; but only its afterglow, 'the back,' so to speak. It is, of course, quite impossible to penetrate the full mystery of these words, conveying sublime truths concerning the Divine nature in the ordinary language of man. Many interpreters deduce from this passage the teaching that no living being can see God's face, *i.e.* penetrate His eternal essence. It is only from the *rearward* that we can know Him. Even as a ship sails through the waters of an ocean and leaves its wake behind, so the Almighty and Most High God may be known by His Divine 'footprints' in human history, by His traces in the human soul.

Before closing the book on Moses, let us first point out two additional facts about him. One author speaks of him on this wise: **"Of all human beings, the one who has most influenced the others is Moses,"** and the author continues, saying that **"it was he [Moses] who discovered the personality of God"** (Exodus 34:6-8).

More than three thousand years ago he was buried "in a valley in the land of Moab," yet his era is only now ending, if indeed it will ever end.

♦♦♦♦♦♦♦♦♦♦♦♦♦♦♦♦♦

The Glory and Beauty of the Hebrew Scriptures continues in the immortal words of two great kings of Israel, the mother of a stalwart prophet, and a woman from the land of Moab who embraced the God of Israel.

THE GLORY & BEAUTY OF THE PSALMS OF DAVID

WHEN THE NAME DAVID king of Israel is mentioned, what is the first thing that comes to mind? Is it his slaying of Goliath? his contribution to humanity of nearly half of the 150 psalms in the scriptures? the matter of Bathsheba and Uriah the Hittite? or his ever penitent spirit and willingness to seek forgiveness for his iniquities?

Whatever the answer, David, despite his many transgressions, was one of the great kings of biblical times and was beloved by his God. Speaking of his iniquities, we never see anywhere in the scriptures where he committed the same sin twice, and was always willing to confess, ask forgiveness and repent, proclaiming:

"I will declare mine iniquity; I will be sorry for my sin."
-- (Psa. 38:18)

Of the 150 psalms in scripture, only 74 are attributed to David. Others were written by Moses (one, the 90th), Solomon, Ethan, and Asaph; the rest are anonymous.

Psalm 119 probably was not written by David, but its uniqueness deserves commentary. It contains 176 verses, and after every eight verses there is a different Hebrew letter, corresponding to the 22 letters of the Hebrew alphabet. After the first eight verses is the first letter, an **aleph** (א) (sometimes spelled **alef;** pronounced **älĕf**). (As stated in the Foreword, we will present additional information on the Hebrew alphabet and a few important self-pronouncing Hebrew words and phrases later on in the book.)

Psalm 119 is the longest passage in the entire Bible. The other interesting aspect about this psalm is that all of its 176 verses, with the exception of seven, make reference to the commandments, statutes, judgments, precepts, law, or word of God. Notice also that the word *chapter* does not appear at the head of each psalm; hence it is unscholarly to say "Psalm chapter 1," etc., but simply "Psalm 1," or "the First Psalm."

Some books of the Hebrew Scriptures are written in poetry, Job and Psalms among them. Poetry in scripture may be difficult to recognize because eastern hemispheric poetry does not rhyme, it contrasts. When two opposing thoughts are expressed in the same verse, or when two statements say the same thing but in different words, these are examples of biblical poetry. Job 8:20 is poetry, and reads thusly:

> *"Behold, God will not cast away a perfect man,*
> *neither will He help the evildoers."*

Psalm 27:1 is another example of biblical poetry:

> *"The LORD is my light and my salvation; whom shall I fear?*
> *The LORD is the strength of my life; of whom shall I be afraid?"*

The 23rd Psalm is believed to be the most comforting of all scriptural passages, and was penned by King David.

There are words of admonition spoken by the Most High to David in the Book of II Samuel (23:1-3), which, though probably little known, are food for thought and great advice for those in positions of authority:

> [1]*"Now these be the last words of David. David the son of Jesse said, and the man who was raised up on high, the anointed of the God of Jacob, and the sweet psalmist of Israel, said,* [2]*The Spirit of the LORD spake by me, and His word was in my tongue. The God of Israel said, the Rock of Israel spake to me,* [3]'*He that ruleth over men must be just, ruling in the fear of God.' "*

Among other glorious and beautiful Psalms are the 1st, 8th, 15th, 37th, 51st, 100th, 136th, and 150th.

SOLOMON'S PROVERBS & ECCLESIASTES
His Wisdom, His Sayings & What Was Said of Him

King Solomon, son of David and third king of Israel, was the wisest of all the kings and the others of his day. He asked the Almighty neither for riches nor for the death of his enemies, but for a wise and understanding heart to lead the people of the Most High God.

David had made all the preparations for the building of the Temple, and 480 years after the children of Israel had come out of the land of Egypt Solomon began to build the house of the Lord. It took seven years to complete.

Solomon's wisdom was unsurpassed, and was to forever be, according to the word of the Most High God (in I Kings 3:12-13):

> [12]*"Behold, I have done according to thy words: lo, I have given thee a wise and understanding heart; so that there was none like thee before thee, neither after thee shall any arise like unto thee.* [13]*And I have also given thee that which thou hast not asked, both riches, and honour: so that there shall not be any among the kings like unto thee all thy days."*

Some of the greatest pearls of wisdom and sound advice found anywhere are in the Books of Proverbs and Ecclesiastes. These four admirable passages from Proverbs are essentially relative to the times in which we now live:

> Proverbs 4:14-17 - *"Enter not into the path of the wicked, and go not in the way of evil men. Avoid it, pass not by it, turn from it, and pass away. For they sleep not, except they have done mischief; and their sleep is taken away, unless they cause some to fall. For they eat the bread of wickedness, and drink the wine of violence."*

> 6:16-19 - [16]*"These six things doth the LORD hate: yea, seven are an abomination unto Him:* [17]*A proud look, a lying tongue, and hands that shed innocent blood,* [18]*An heart that deviseth wicked imaginations, feet that be swift in running to mischief,* [19]*A false witness that speaketh lies, and he that soweth discord*

among brethren."

16:18 - *"Pride goeth before destruction, and an haughty spirit before a fall."*

30:11 - *"There is a generation that curseth their father, and doth not bless their mother."*

As we continue to explore *the Glory and Beauty of the Hebrew Scriptures,* we now come to the Book of *Ecclesiastes,* from the Hebrew *Koheleth,* **the Preacher.** Like the Book of Proverbs, Ecclesiastes, too, is filled with golden nuggets of wisdom, knowledge and understanding. We begin with 3:11:

(From the Hebrew Holy Scriptures)
"He [the Creator] *hath made everything beautiful in its time; also He hath set the world in their heart, yet so that man cannot find out the work that God hath done from the beginning even to the end."*

8:11 - *"Because sentence against an evil work is not executeth speedily, therefore the heart of the sons of men is fully set in them to do evil."*

8:17 - *"Then I beheld all the work of God, that man cannot find out the work that is done under the sun; because though a man labour to seek it out, yet he shall not find it; yea further, though a wise man think to know it, yet shall he not be able to find it."*

10:18 - *"By much slothfulness the building decayeth; and through idleness of the hands the house droppeth through."*

In Ecclesiastes 3:1-8 we are reminded that there is a time to every purpose under the heaven; this chapter makes for some of the most excellent reading.

HANNAH PRAYS FOR A SON

One of the most moving passages in the scriptures is found in I Samuel chapters 1 and 2 – that of Hannah, wife of Elkanah.

Now Elkanah had two wives, Hannah and Peninnah. Peninnah had children – sons and daughters – but Hannah was barren. Peninnah provoked Hannah to the point where she was saddened, she cried, and would not eat. Elkanah loved Hannah and tried to cheer her by saying to her, "Why eatest thou not? and why is thy heart grieved? am I not better to thee than ten sons?" But Hannah would not be comforted.

When time came for the family to go up to Shiloh to offer the yearly sacrifice, Elkanah gave his wives and children goodly portions to offer and gave to Hannah an extra portion. Yet no amount of tangible gifts or kind words could bring joy to the heart of Hannah, only a son.

Shiloh (*place of rest*) was a city 17 miles north of Jerusalem and was the center of Israelite worship before Jerusalem was chosen. One year when Hannah went up to offer to the Lord she decided to fervently pray for a son from the Most High God. Eli was the high priest of the time, and when he saw her standing at the altar with her lips moving but no sound being uttered, he chided her vehemently, thinking that she was drunk. He said to Hannah, who was praying and weeping in the bitterness of her soul unto the Lord:

> I Samuel 1:14-16 - [14]*"And Eli said unto her, How long wilt thou be drunken? Put away thy wine from thee.* [15]*And Hannah answered and said, No, my lord, I am a woman of a sorrowful spirit: I have drunk neither wine nor strong drink, but have poured out my soul unto the LORD. Count not thine handmaid for a daughter of Belial: for out of the abundance of my complaint and grief have I spoken hitherto."*

In her prayer she requested of the Almighty and Most High God that He would grant her the gift of a son. And she vowed a vow, saying,

"O Lord of hosts, if Thou wilt indeed look on the affliction of thine handmaid, and remember me, and not forget thine handmaid, but wilt give unto thine handmaid a man child, then I will give him unto the LORD all the days of his life, and there shall no razor come upon his head."

Hannah's prayer was answered, and she bore a son and called his name Samuel, which means, *asked of God.*

HANNAH'S PRAYER OF THANKSGIVING

I Sam. 2:1-10 - And Hannah prayed, and said, *"My heart rejoiceth in the LORD, mine horn is exalted in the LORD: my mouth is enlarged over mine enemies; because I rejoice in Thy salvation. ²There is none holy as the LORD: for there is none beside Thee: neither is there any rock like our God. ³Talk no more so exceeding proudly; let not arrogancy come out of your mouth: for thr LORD is a God of knowledge, and by Him actions are weighed. ⁴The bows of the mighty men are broken, and they that stumbled are girded with strength. ⁵They that were full have hired out themselves for bread, and they that were hungry ceased: so that the barren hath born seven; and she that hath many children is waxed feeble. ⁶The LORD killeth, and maketh alive: He bringeth down to the grave, and bringeth up. ⁷The LORD maketh poor, and maketh rich: He bringeth low, and lifteth up. ⁸He raiseth up the poor out of the dust, and lifteth up the beggar from the dunghill, to set them among princes, and to make them inherit the throne of glory: for the pillars of the earth are the LORD's, and He hath set the world upon them. ⁹He will keep the feet of His saints, and the wicked shall be silent in darkness; for by strength shall no man prevail. ¹⁰The adversaries of the LORD shall be broken to pieces; out of heaven shall He thunder upon them: the LORD shall judge the ends of the earth; and He shall give strength unto His king, and exalt the horn of His anointed."*

"The child Samuel grew on," say the scriptures, "and was in favour both with the LORD, and also with men." Hannah, who had been barren, not only gave birth to Samuel, but became the mother of five more sons and daughters. Samuel then went on to become a great prophet in Israel, so much so that the scripture speaks thusly of him (I Sam. 3:19):

"And Samuel grew, and the LORD was with him, and did let none of his words fall to the ground."

Because Hannah poured out her soul to the Almighty in the bitterness of her spirit, there came to be a prophet named Samuel. Had she not prayed, millions throughout today's world propably would not be bearing the name *Samuel,* for he is the only *Samuel* in all of scripture. Hallelujah! Hallelujah! Hannah prayed!

———————

As we continue our dissertation under the heading, *THE GLORY & BEAUTY OF THE HEBREW SCRIPTURES,* there are just three more champions of righteousness within the pages of the *Tanakh* (O.T.) upon whom we will focus, without whose immortal words this section would not be complete. They are: Ruth and Naomi (as one), the Prophet Jeremiah, and the Prophet Micah.

Of the books of the Hebrew Scriptures named for people, two of them were not Hebrews/Israelites/Jews. One was Ruth of the land of Moab (in the Dead Sea region), and the other Jōb, from the land of Uz of Arabia. Our concentration at this time is on Ruth and her mother-in-law, Naomi.

RUTH THE MOABITESS & NAOMI THE ISRAELITE

THERE WAS A FAMINE IN BETHLEHEM-JUDAH where Elimelech and his wife Naomi lived. Therefore, they and their two sons, Mahlon and Chilion, decided to migrate to Moab for the sake of survival.

Not long thereafter Elimelech died, and Naomi was left with just her two sons. They married women of Moab; Chilion married Orpah, and Mahlon Ruth. Naomi not only witnessed the death of her husband, but soon both her sons also died, leaving Orpah and Ruth widows. All this took place within a ten-year period, the length of time which Naomi spent in Moab. Left to fend for themselves were three widows, Naomi and her two daughters-in-law; how crushed they must have felt with life dealing them such a treacherous blow. Word had spread from country to country that the famine in Judæa had ended, *"and how that the* LORD *had visited His people in giving them bread"* (Ruth 1:6). With no biological family left in Moab, Naomi decided to return to Bethlehem, accompanied by her daughters-in-law. Naomi time after time tried to persuade them to return to their own land, their own people and their gods, but they insisted on accompanying Naomi back to her home in Bethlehem-Judah. In Ruth 1:8-15, Naomi gives good reason why her two daughters-in-law should leave her and return home:

"And Naomi said unto her two daughters in law, Go, return each to her mother's house: the LORD *deal kindly with you, as ye have dealt with the dead, and with me. The* LORD *grant you that ye may find rest, each of you in the house of her husband. Then she kissed them: and they lifted up their voice and wept. And they said unto her, Surely we will return with thee to thy people. And Naomi said, Turn again, my daughters: why will ye go with me? Are there yet any more sons in my womb, that they may be your husbands? Turn again, my daughters, go your way; for I am too old to have a husband, If I should say, I have hope, if I should have an husband also to-night, and should also bear sons; would ye tarry for them until they were grown? Would ye stay for them from having husbands? Nay, my daughters; for it grieveth me much for your sakes that the hand of the* LORD *is gone out against me. And they lifted up their voice, and wept again: and Orpah kissed her mother in law; but Ruth clave unto her. And she said, Behold thy sister in law is gone back unto her people, and unto her gods: return thou after thy sister in law."*

Naomi pressed and pressed, but to no avail, in the case of Ruth. Up to this point Naomi had by far been doing most of the talking, but now Ruth's chance had arrived to have her name indelibly inscribed in the pages of holy scripture, though never did she know. Her endearing, immortal words have rung down through the corridors of time, and help make up **the Glory and Beauty of the Hebrew Scriptures:**

> (Ruth 1:16-17) *And Ruth said* [to Naomi], *"Entreat me not to leave thee, or to return from following after thee: for whither thou goest, I will go; and where thou lodgest, I will lodge: thy people shall be my people, and thy God my God: Where thou diest, will I die, and there will I be buried: the LORD do so to me, and more also, if aught but death part thee and me."*

What a love story! I ask, rhetorically, did a greater love ever exist than between Ruth and Naomi?

Naomi had become a weary, wayworn woman, having escaped a famine in her homeland and experienced the death of three loved ones on foreign soil. Life's many burdens had taken an awful toll on her, both physically and emotionally. We can see by the eye of faith how that Naomi had aged considerably, her hair had turned to silver, and there was a noticeable bend in the area of her shoulders. What was once a beautiful woman in her youth in Bethlehem had now become a toddling widow with the appearance of one much older than her years. The people of Bethlehem scarcely knew her, for upon her return they inquired, "Is this Naomi?" She speaks of having become afflicted (Ruth 1:20-21):

> (And she said unto them) *"Call me not *Naomi, call me *Mara: for the Almighty hath dealt very bitterly with me. I went out full, and the LORD hath brought me home again empty: why then call ye me Naomi, seeing the LORD hath testified against me, and the Almighty hath afflicted me?"*

Life had been no bed of roses for neither Naomi nor Ruth. The Almighty and Most High Creator has a way of sometimes leading His own in a round-about way – a way in which they know not. Yet, in the end, the perilous and troubling experiences often suffered by the righteous almost always ultimately

---

*Mara means *bitter. *Naomi means *my delight.

lead to a glorious victory. Notice in the unfolding of events that follow how they all worked out for the greater good. Naomi had a kinsmans of her late husband in the suburbs of Bethlehem named Boaz, a mighty man of wealth. She encouraged Ruth to go and work in the fields of Boaz. When he noticed her, he inquired of one of his servants, "Who is the damsel?", and he informed him that she was Ruth of Moab who had returned with Naomi. Her beauty and virtuousness won his heart, and he gave her a choice place with the rest of his maidens. Actually, Boaz was a near kinsman to Naomi's deceased husband Elimelech, and Naomi and Elimelech's deceased son Mahlon was Ruth's husband. In fact, Naomi refers to Boaz, in 2:20, as *"near of kin to us"* and *"one of our next kinsmen."* Boaz, who grew to love Ruth, felt obligated to marry her to raise up seed to his kinsman, according to the law in Israel. They continued showing tender lovingkindness one to another, with Boaz giving orders to his servants to bestow extra favors upon Ruth.

According to the account recorded in Ruth 4:13, Boaz and Ruth married, and she conceived and bore a son:

> *"So Boaz took Ruth, and she was his wife: and when he went in unto her, the LORD gave her conception, and she bare a son."*

The son was named Obed, with Naomi becoming his nurse. One may ask, "Just what is the blessing in this long string of earlier misfortunes? It is this: Obed was the father of Jesse, and Jesse was the father of David, king of Israel. Ruth the Moabitess, then, was the great-grandmother of David.

Read the Book of Ruth; it is one of the most touching in scripture. Surely, the words of the prophets are true: *". . . There is no searching of His understanding . . ."* and *"God is great, and we know Him not . . ."* It was this awesome Almighty Power who suffered the lives of Naomi and Ruth to be turned completely upside down with heartache, pain and woe, that He might bring them out more than conquerors and also accomplish His purposes. With all that Naomi endured, we find nowhere in the annals of her life that she charged the Almighty foolishly. The least she said of Him was that *"the hand of the LORD is gone out against me,"* and *"the Almighty hath dealt very bitterly with me."* Both she and Ruth kept a humble spirit toward their Maker, and after riding out the storms of life, they then long enjoyed the blesings of a merciful and loving Redeemer.

The moral: Trust! Obey! Wait . . . till the change comes!

THE PROPHET JEREMIAH

(Pronounced "JER'-E-**MI**'-A." Definition: "Whom Yahweh has appointed." In Hebrew, "Yir'-me-**yä**'-hu.")

JEREMIAH BEGAN HIS PROPHECY TO ISRAEL in 626 B.C.E. For 42 years he warned the inhabitants, foretelling the impending destruction of Jerusalem by Nebuchadnezzar and the Babylonian army, if Israel did not return to works of righteousness. His prophecy for the most part went unheeded, and in 588 B.C.E. the siege of Jerusalem began. Thousands, mainly of the tribes of Judah and Benjamin, were thrust into Babylonian captivity and carried away to the land of the Chaldeans.

The purpose of this segment of the book is not to give a historical account of the life of Jeremiah and the Israelites of his day, but to continue bringing to light *the glory and beauty of the Hebrew Scriptures.*

Within the Book of Jeremiah are contained scores of beautiful and glorious passages spoken by the Prophet. Some of these passages are revelations from the Most High God, others are the prophet's own expressions of his feelings about his mission. His revelations from the Almighty are invariably prefaced with such phrases as, *"Moreover the word of the LORD came to me, saying, . . .";* *"Hear ye the word which the LORD speaketh unto you, O house of Israel . . .";* *"Thus saith the LORD unto me . . .,"* etc. This consistency runs throughout the messages of all the prophets in the Hebrew Scriptures (O.T.); however, none of the messages within the confines of the Greek Scriptures (N.T.) are undergirded with the phrase *"thus saith the* LORD *God,"* or its equivalent.

For those seeking a way of life to embrace and the criteria by which to guage it, we offer the following, from Jeremiah 6:16:

> *"Thus saith the* LORD, *Stand ye in the ways, and see, and ask for the old paths, where is the good way, and walk therein, and ye shall find rest for your souls. But they said, We will not walk therein."*

Jeremiah the prophet possessed a very deep love and concern for his people, the children of Israel. He desired desperately to reach them with his words, but the masses rejected him, even though his messages were directly from the Almighty and Most High God, through the medium of Divine revelation.

This author sympathizes with the Prophet, realizing full well how difficult it is, if not impossible, to reach a people who just don't believe. Jeremiah's tears were his meat day and night, not for himself but for Israel. Listen to his plea in their behalf, from 8:20-22, and 9:1 (KJV):

> [20]*"The harvest is past, the summer is ended, and we are not saved.* [21]*For the hurt of the daughter of my people am I hurt; I am black; astonishment hath taken hold on me.* [22]*Is there no balm in Gilead? Is there no physician there? why then is not the health of the daughter of my people recovered?"* [9:1] *"O that my head were waters, and mine eyes a fountain of tears, that I might weep day and night for the slain of the daughter of my people!"*

As you read such passages in holy scripture, and many others akin to them, cannot you see that they point directly to the present condition and predicament of our people? As it was with the people of the Most High in the days of the prophet Jeremiah, so it is with us today. Thousands within the Hebrew-Israelite community are in pain, as was the Prophet, as we discern that True Israel has forgotten and forsaken the commandments of the Almighty Creator and has engaged himself in the worship of the slavemaster's false god.

As many in ancient Israel under Jeremiah began to glory and trust in the arm of flesh, the Most High admonished them thusly (9:23-24):

> [23] *"Thus saith the LORD, Let not the wise man glory in his wisdom, neither let the mighty man glory in his might, let not the rich man glory in his riches;* [24]*But let him that glorieth glory in this, that he understandeth and knowest Me, that I am the LORD which exercise lovingkindness, judgment, and righteousness, in the earth: for in these things I delight, saith the LORD."*

Ofttimes Jeremiah became discouraged. Certainly, within the 42 years of his prophecy, considering his set of circumstances, despondency would set in from time to time. However, the Prophet kept the Most High before him, and managed to always muster up enough spiritual strength to encourage himself in the Lord his God. In 15:16, he proclaims the rejoicing and joy within his heart, saying:

> *"Thy words were found, and I did eat them; and Thy word was unto me the joy and rejoicing of mine heart: for I am called by Thy name, O LORD God of hosts."*

The **Glory and Beauty of the Hebrew Scriptures** are endless, as we now call attention to Jer. 17:5-7:

> [5]*"Thus saith the LORD, Cursed be the man that trusteth in man, and maketh flesh his arm, and whose heart departeth from the LORD.* [6]*For he shall be like the heath in the desert, and shall not see when good cometh . . .;* [7]**Blessed is the man that trusteth in the LORD, and whose hope the LORD is."**

In 17:14, the Prophet prays for healing, probably both physical and spiritual:

> *"Heal me, O LORD, and I shall be healed; save me, and I shall be saved: for Thou art my praise."*

There were many false prophets among the people of Israel in the Prophet's day, therefore, he must have fully realized that if he, the only true prophet, were to crumble under the pressures of his foes, then wickedness would become victorious. He remembered the words of his Creator, who had earlier revealed to him this message of hope: *"Blessed is the man that trusteth in the LORD, and whose hope the LORD is."* In this he strengthened himself, took fresh courage and continued to trust in his Almighty Saviour.

One of the many places in scripture which describes the Most High God as "close-up and personal," so to speak, appears in the Book of Jeremiah. In this passage the Almighty causes us to know that He is not some distant Being "way beyond the sun" (which is 93 million miles away), but is omnipresent – everywhere at the same time – and is the Almighty Eternal Universal Power. A scripture supporting His omnipotence, omnipresence and omniscience is Jer. 23:23-24:

[23] *"Am I a God at hand, saith the LORD, and not a God afar off?* [24]*Can any hide himself in secret places that I shall not see him? saith the LORD. <u>Do not I fill heaven and earth? saith the LORD.</u>"*

The Bible speaks hundreds of times of "God being in heaven." Literally this is not so (since neither heaven nor hell are geographical locations), but can best be explained in the prayer of David in I Chronicles 29:11 (last portion):

". . . Thine is the kingdom, O LORD, <u>and Thou art exalted as head above all.</u>"

Do not think *"God is in heaven"*; think *"God is exalted as head above all."* For if the Almighty and Most High is in heaven – and in heaven alone – then where was He before heaven was created, if Genesis 1:1 is true, which states, *"In the beginning <u>God created the heaven</u> and the earth"?* The prophet Zephaniah concurs (in 3:17):

"The LORD thy God <u>in the midst of thee</u> is mighty; He will save, He will rejoice over thee with joy . . ."

The Prophet probably reached the lowest point in his entire prophetic career, when he entertained the thought not to speak in God's name any more, due to the mistreatment from the segment of the people who were his enemies. Poor Jeremiah! He pours out his soul in anguish and despair (20:7-9, Hebrew Holy Scriptures):

> [7]*"O LORD, Thou hast enticed me, and I was enticed, Thou hast overcome me, and hast prevailed; I am become a laughing-stock all the day, every one mocketh me.* [8]*For as often as I speak, I cry out, I cry: 'Violence and spoil'; because the word of the LORD is made a repraoch unto me, and a derision, all the day.* [9]**And if I say, 'I will not make mention of Him, nor speak any more in His name,' then there is in my heart as it were a burning fire shut up in my bones, and I weary myself to hold it in, but cannot.**"

The prophet Jeremiah, fearful of experiencing a feeling which he described as *"a burning fire shut up in my bones,"* if he were to refrain from prophesying in God's name, decided to continue trying to save Israel from Babylonin Captivity. But at last, he could not. He stood with tears in his eyes for nearly two years and watched the Chaldeans invade and finally destroy Jerusalem, and carry thousands of his fellow Israelites off to Babylon for seventy years of exile.

WISDOM OF THE ALMIGHTY THROUGH THE PROPHET MICAH

MICAH THE PROPHET began his prophecy in circa 750 B.C.E., during the reigns of Jotham, Ahaz, and Hezekiah. Among other things, Micah speaks out against both animal and human sacrifice. He also admonishes of the danger of putting one's ultimate trust in flesh, and of the Most High's saving power and His willingness to pardon our iniquities. We begin with the prohibition of sacrifices and the three major things which the Almighty requires (Micah 6:6-8):

[6]*"Wherewith shall I come before the LORD, and bow myself before the high God? Shall I come before Him with burnt offerings, with calves of a year old?* [7]*Will the LORD be pleased with thousands of rams, or with ten thousands of rivers of oil? Shall I give my firstborn for my transgression, the fruit of my body for the sin of my soul?* [8]*He hath showed thee, O man, what is good; and what doth the LORD require of thee, but to do justly, and to love mercy, and to walk humbly with thy God?"*

Humans are limited and temporary, the Prophet warns; only the Almighty is limitless and Eternal. From Micah 7:5-7 we offer the following:

[5]*"Trust ye not in a friend, put ye not confidence in a guide; Keep the doors of thy mouth from her that lieth in thy bosom.* [6]*For the son dishonoureth the father, the daughter riseth up against her mother, the daughter in law against her mother in law; a man's enemies are the men of his own house.* [7]*Therefore I will look unto the LORD; I will wait for the God of my salvation: my God will hear me."*

And lastly, the prophet Micah closes his prophecy, leaving us with hope and promise that the Eternal One, blessed be He, is merciful, will forgive our sins, and will cast them into the sea of forgetfulness to remember them no more. From chapter 7:18-20, we are heartened:

[18]*"Who is a God like unto Thee, who pardoneth iniquity, and passeth by the transgression of the remnant of His heritage? He retaineth not His anger for ever, because He delighteth in mercy.* [19]*He will turn again, He will have compassion upon us; He will subdue our iniquities; and Thou wilt cast all their sins into the depths of the sea.* [20]*Thou wilt perform the truth to Jacob, and the mercy to Abraham, which Thou hast sworn unto our fathers from the days of old."*

As we bring to a close this section of the book under the heading, **The Glory and Beauty of the Hebrew Scriptures,** we trust that this journey through the Tanakh (O.T.) of selected passages has been a most rewarding experience.

Despite the ungodly acts committed by many during the so-called 'Old Testament' period, that does not negate the fact that thousands of holy and righteous men and women purposed in their hearts to "walk and talk with God." Certainly the pearls of wisdon and the full and sufficient guide to righteousness found in the pages of The Holy Scriptures far outnumber and outweigh the iniquities and abominations of those who chose to walk in the ways of degradation and to sell themselves to work evil. The Righteous – Be They Ever Blessed!!

~~~~~~

"He who's forced against his will is of the same opinion still."

———————————

"The heart cannot condone what the mind condemns."

AS YOU CONTINUE TO READ THIS BOOK, YOU WILL SEE WHY WE VEHEMENTLY CONTEND (AND WILL DEBATE ANYONE ON THE MATTER) THAT "THE HEBREW SCRIPTURES" (O.T.) AND "THE GREEK SCRIPTURES" (N.T.) SHOULD NOT BE UNDER THE SAME COVER, AS THEY ARE TWO DIFFERENT SCRIPTURES. CHRISTIANITY WOULD HAVE YOU BELIEVE THAT THE GREEK SCRIPTURES ARE A FULFILLMENT OF THE HEBREW SCRIPTURES, BUT THEY ARE NOT! THIS IS PART OF THE NEAR-1900-YEAR-OLD DECEPTION. DON'T BE FOOLED!!

CHAPTER 3

The Greek Scriptures (NT): Similarities & Dissimilarities to the Hebrew Scriptures (OT)

THE MESSAGES OF THE GREEK SCRIPTRES fall within four categories: the True, the False, the Credible, and the Incredible. Rather than write separately in each of these divisions, we will interweave our findings simultaneously as we progress through the various passages of the Christian scriptures, which have been compiled and canonized by the Greeks, the Romans, and the Roman Catholic Church.

The Greek Scriptures (N.T.) are greatly dependent upon the Hebrew Scriptures (O.T.). The following statistic is both little known and startling: Within the Greek Scriptures – which contain 27 books, from Matthew to Revelation – there are 484 quotations which have been extracted from the Hebrew Scriptures, without which the Greek Scriptures could not be complete and probably would not exist.

Yeshua (Jesus) very often quoted from "The Law" (Torah: Genesis through Deuteronomy), "The Prophets," and "The Psalms." Those books of the Greek Scriptures, aside from the four Gospels, which have been attributed to Yeshua's disciples, such as *The Epistle of James* and *The First* and *Second Epistles of Peter,* also depend largely upon the Hebrew Scriptures for their content. The Epistles of Saul (now known as the Apostle Paul) run the gamut almost from Adam to Malachi, and the Book of Revelation is no exception; it is quite repetitive with references from Isaiah, Daniel, Ezekiel, Zechariah, and other contributors to the Hebrew Scriptures.

It must be borne in mind that the Greek Scriptures did not exist during the times of Yeshua and his disciples, Paul, *Luke, or John the Revelator. The only scriptures that they and the people of their times had were the Hebrew Scriptures. †"The Greek Scriptures were written within the first century after Yeshua, but two or three more centuries passed before the Canon was finally settled. This was done by the councils of Laodicea (A.D. 369), Hippo Regius (A.D. 393), and Carthage (A.D. 397)."

The Greek Scriptures, though not written by Yeshua or during his lifetime but many, many decades later, exist for the purpose of exalting and magnifying him as the savior of the world. This concept is not the teaching of Yeshua, but of Paul (the self-proclaimed apostle to the Gentiles), the Roman Catholic Church, Emperor Constantine of Rome and the Nicene Council of 325 C.E. (A.D.). Although a great portion of the Greek Scriptures is quoted from the Hebrew Scriptures, their paramount teachings are not in harmony with the Divine Revelations of Moses, the prophets and others whom they quote. Much of what they have used has been taken out of context, with the intent to deceive and to create the new man-made religion of Christianity.

It is amazingly incredible for a compilation of sacred scriptures of any religion to use 484 quotations from another persuasion, and yet does not make the God of that persuasion the center of its message. To prove that the Most High God is the secondary subject of the Greek Scriptures, consider the following comparisons:

The word *God* (in reference to the Creator of the universe) appears in the Hebrew Scriptures a total of 3,028 times. In the Greek Scriptures, which has only 12 books less than the HS, the word *God* (in reference to the Creator of the universe) ap-

---

*Luke, a Greek, was not a disciple of Yeshua, but Paul's companion. Neither saw Yeshua.

†According to Philip Schaff, DD., LLD, professor of Church History, Union Theological Seminary, New York, NY.

pears 1,317 times. Similarly, the word *LORD* (as it applies to the Creator) appears more than 6,900 times in the Hebrew Scriptures. *Lord* appears in the Greek Scriptures 711 times; 692 of those times it applies to Yeshua, and only 19 times to the Creator. Three examples of the hundreds of times that "Lord" is used in the Greek Scriptures and applies to Yeshua (Jesus) are Luke 2:11 and I Thessalonians 4:16-17:

> (Luke 2:11) *"For unto you is born this day in the city of David a Saviour, which is Christ the <u>Lord.</u>"*

> (I Thess. 4:16-17) *"For the <u>Lord</u> himself shall descend from heaven with a shout, with the voice of the archangel. . . .Then we . . . shall be caught up to meet the <u>Lord</u> in the air . . ."*

Both these passages are in disharmony with the Tanakh (O.T.), because the Most High declares in Isaiah 42:8 (and in more than 100 other places in the Tanakh – OT):

> *"<u>I am 'the LORD': that is My name:</u> and My glory will I not give to another, neither My praise to graven images."*

Now let us cite some statistics on the number of times that *Christ, Jesus Christ, Jesus,* and *Christ Jesus* are listed in the Greek Scriptures: Combined, they appear for a total of 1,465 times, 148 more times than does the word "God." From these figures we can readily see that the main emphasis of the Greek Scriptures is not on the Almighty God, but on Jesus Christ.

Yet, **the Lawgiver Moses,** probably the most prominent figure in the entire Hebrew Scriptures, **is recorded a total of 733 times,** and *God* and *LORD* combine for a total of 9,928 times. *Moses* is mentioned in the Greek Scriptures 80 times.

In all the above conclusions, consideration has not been given to the many pronouns for God (*I, He, His, Him, Thee, Thou, Thine,* etc.) and to such terms as *Almighty, Most High, Creator, Maker,* etc., which appear within the volume of the Tanakh (O.T.). Neither have we taken into account the scores of times that the word *Father* and other pronouns for God are used by Yeshua (Jesus) and other (NT) contributors.

There is a problem with the word *Lord* the way it appears in the Greek Scriptures: There is no distinction made when it applies to the Creator and when it applies to the Christian "Lord Jesus," who was a mortal man. In both instances it is rendered "Lord." In Yeshua's (Jesus') parables, however, a difference is made in his use of the word *lord,* and is used in the following example to describe an authority figure:

> *"Blessed is that servant whom when his lord shall come, shall find him so doing."*

The Hebrew Scriptures in all of its books make the distinction in this way: "LORD" and "LORD" are only for the Creator of the universe, and "lord" is for a man in authority. (For examples of the use of "LORD," see Genesis chapter 2.)

___

WAS YESHUA's TEACHING CONSISTENT WITH THAT OF THE PROPHETS IN THE TANAKH (O.T.)?

We have long been of the opinion that the Divine Hand had to have been at work during the Greek Scriptures' compilation and canonization, else those who wrote it would have been able to make incontestable the many discrepancies and deliberate deceptions contained in the four Gospels and in the epistles of the Apostle Paul.

Were it not for some of the true teaching of Yeshua in Matthew, Mark, Luke, and John, there would be substantial grounds for us to disregard most of the Greek Scripture's writings. We are very aware that there are many sayings that the compilers say that Yeshua said that he did not really say. These Gentile insertions will be brought to the attention of the reader in the next chapter. **Nevertheless, because Yeshua gave credence time after time to Moses, the Law, and the Prophets, we therefore applaud and will also cite many of those instances in this chapter.**

In Answer to the Question

Yeshua ben Yosef (which by interpretation is, Joshua son of Joseph) was a Hebrew Israelite prophet of and for his day, and was addressed on six different occasions in the Greek Scrip- tures as *Rabbi,* which means *master; teacher of Torah.* Therefore, as a teacher of Torah, Yeshua's prophecy was consistent with that of the prophets from Moses to Malachi. In Matthew 5:17-19 Yeshua upholds the teachings of the Law and the Prophets, saying:

[17] *"Think not that I am come to destroy the law, or the prophets: I am not come to destroy, but to fulfill.* [18]*For verily I say unto you, Till heaven and earth pass, one jot or one tittle shall in no wise pass from the law, till all be fulfilled.* [19]*Whosoever therefore shall break one of these least commandments, and shall teach men so, he shall be called the least in the kingdom of heaven: but whosoever shall do and teach them, the same shall be called great in the kingdom of heaven. "*

In Matthew 7:12 Yeshua attributes the Golden Rule as having had its origin in the Law and the Prophets of the Hebrew Scriptures:

"Therefore all things whatsoever ye would that men should do to you, do ye even so to them: for this is the law and the prophets, " (Or, in other words, as the Golden Rule has come down to us through the years, *"Do unto others as you would have them do unto you. "*)

In Mark 12:29-30, Yeshua is found teaching from Deuter- onomy 6:4-5 and Leviticus 19:18:

[29]*"The first of all the commandments is, Hear, O Israel; the Lord our God is one Lord:* [30]*And thou shalt love the Lord thy God with all thy heart, and with all thy soul, and with all thy mind, and with all thy strength: this is the first commandment. And the second is like, namely this, Thou shalt love thy neighbor as thyself. There is none other commandment greater than these. "*

From the Book of Genesis, Yeshua makes mention in very favorable ways of righteous Abel (Mt. 23:35); Noah (Mt. 24:

37-39), and Abraham, Isaac, and Jacob (Mt. 8:11, 12:26). Yeshua gives credence to Abraham, father of the faithful, in 16 other places in the *Gospels* section of the Greek Scriptures.

In addition, we find that Yeshua applauded the works of the Lawgiver Moses, Jōb, David, Solomon, the prophets Isaiah, Jeremiah, Daniel, and Jonah. Yeshua was blessed while an infant by the priest Simeon, frequently attended Sabbath services at the synagogue in Nazareth, and often entered into the temple when in Jerusalem. He never attended a church, as there was none in existence in his day. Yeshua also memorialized the exodus of the children of Israel from Egyptian bondage by keeping the feast of the LORD's Passover, and even honored one of the minor Israelite observances, the Feast of the Dedication, according to the record of John 10:22-23. Some Greek Scripture historians have concluded that this was the celebration of Hanukah, an event which took place in 165 B.C.E., when the Maccabean revolt against the Syrians and the Greeks restored the worship to the Temple.

So the conclusion is that Yeshua's teaching was consistent with that of the Hebrew prophets of the Tanakh (O.T.), and that he was born a Hebrew-Israelite, and lived and died a Hebrew-Israelite.

CHAPTER 4

Red-letter Edition Bibles:

DID YESHUA (Jesus) REALLY SAY THAT?

RED-LETTER EDITION BIBLES claim to carry the words spoken by Yeshua printed in *red.* We are aware that the 27 books from Matthew to Revelation were written in Greek and later translated into various other languages, including English, and that something is usually lost in any translation. We also realize that Yeshua was not quoting from any of today's common versions when he taught and read from the Hebrew Scriptures, as they were non-existent at the time. An ancient Hebrew manuscript was translated into the Greek Septuagint Version in ca. 284-246 B.C.E. Copies of these Hebrew manuscripts were in use during the time of Yeshua, consisting only of the Tanakh (O.T.).

But are every word, phrase, clause and sentence printed in red in the Greek Scriptures really the words of Yeshua? Or are some of those words and statements actually additions and the influences of the Greeks, the Romans, and the Roman Catholic Church, who compiled and canonized that body of scriptures, with the intent to deceive?

"Eat My Body" and "Drink My Blood"

We will now proceed to quote some of the many passages in the Greek Scriptures that seem highly improbable and very unlikely to have been said by Yeshua. We begin with Matthew 26:26-28; the underscored italicized words are attributed to Yeshua:

[26] "And as they were eating, Jesus took bread, and blessed it, and brake it, and gave it to the disciples, and said, <u>Take, eat, this is my body.</u> [27]And he took the cup, and gave thanks, and gave it to them, saying, <u>Drink ye all of it.</u> [28]<u>For this is my blood of the new testament, which is shed for many for the remission of sins.</u>"

Christianity refers to the above event as "the Last Supper," when clearly it was the annual Feast of the Passover, which happened to be Yeshua's (Jesus') last, according to the four Gospels. It would be more appropriate for Christians to call it *Jesus' Last Passover.* This is one of several cases where Christianity has taken an Israelite holy festival and Christianized it. Pésach (Passover), a time to celebrate Israel's deliverance from Egyptian bondage, c.a. 1491 B.C.E. (Ex. Chap. 12), takes on an altogether new meaning thirty years into the Common Era, and its significance is then shifted to the remembrance of the suffering and death of Yeshua. How odd it is to memorialize the death of someone before he even dies.

The menu at this Passover meal consisted of matzoh (unleavened bread), the Paschal lamb, and water. (Some sources outside the Bible say that wine was served, as well.) Matt. 26: 26 (last part) says, "<u>Take, eat; this is my body.</u>" The Catholic Church believes that the bread and wine served during communion are actually transformed into and literally become Christ's body and blood.

We do not believe that Yeshua would command his disciples to eat his body, not even symbolically. The same is true with the water/wine in Matt. 26:27, 28: *Drink ye all of it. For this is my blood of the new testament, which is shed for many for the remission of sins.* Blood consumption was forbidden by the Almighty from the time of Noah into the Mosaic period and beyond. Yeshua certainly would not have violated these prohibitive commands. These rituals were hold-overs from Egyptian, Babylonian, Greek, and Roman mythological systems, and especially the ceremonies of ancient Persia, where the popular *Mithraic Cult existed before the Sixth Century B.C., and blood was consumed in worship to pagan gods. Influences of Mithraism and other pagan religions are quite visible throughout Christianity.

Of the four Gospels that record Yeshua's last Passover (Mt. 26:28, Mk. 14:24, Lu. 22:20, Jn. ch. 13), Matthew (in 26:28) is the only one that includes the phrase, *for the remission of sins.* Throughout the Hebrew Scriptures the Most High forbids human sacrifice. He would not allow Abraham to offer up his son as a sacrifice; why, then, would the Almighty condone the death of Yeshua or any other human being as a sacrifice for sin? Yeshua was indicted by the Roman government on charges of sedition and blasphemy; they gave him a trial, found him guilty, and put him to death. His sentence was by no means salvational, but political. (For a greater, in-depth understanding on this and other subjects pertaining to Yeshua, obtain a copy of our 'must-read' book entitled *A Non-Christian's Response To Christianity,* 152 pp.).

The phrase *new testament* is used in Matt. 26:28 ("For this is my blood of the new testament"). Certainly this could not possibly be referring to the books of the Greek Scriptures, Matthew through Revelation, as there was no New Testament when the passage in question was written. According to Webster's Collegiate Dictionary, one definition of *testament* is *covenant.* So what Matt. 26:28 is actually saying is, *"this is my blood of the new covenant . . . "* The intent here is to have you believe that Yeshua ushered in a "new covenant," and that the so-called "old covenant" of the Hebrew Scriptures between the Most High God and Israel has now been annuled. This is totally untrue.

The irrevocable covenant which the Almighty God made with Israel is The Ten Commandments, as recorded in Deut. 4:13, Psalm 111:7, 8, and in scores of other places:

---

*Research "Mithra," "Mithras," and "Mithraism" in the encyclopaedia or the internet, and see the parallelisms between them and Christianity.

"And He [YAH] *declared unto you His covenant, which He commanded you to perform, even Ten Commandments, and He wrote them upon two tables of stone."* (Deut. 4:13.)
"The works of His hands are verity and judgment; all His commandments are sure. They stand fast for ever and ever, and are done in truth and uprightness. He sent redemption unto His people: He hath commanded His covenant for ever: holy and reverend is His name. (Psalm 111:7, 8.)

Yeshua would never, neither could he or anyone else ever revoke the Sinaitic covenant between the Most High and Israel. He said (in Matt. 5:17) that he "came not to destroy the law or the prophets."

"Let Him Take Up His *'Cross'*, and Follow Me"

In three of the four Gospels is carried the passage attributed to Yeshua as the criteria for becoming his follower. In the book of Matthew (16:24) is recorded the following:

Then said Jesus unto his disciples, "If any man will come after me, let him deny himself, and take up his cross, and follow me."

Requiring one to "deny himself" in order to become one of Yeshua's followers is quite understandable. But we cannot bring ourselves to believe that he would actually set as a standard for discipleship that one "take up his cross, and follow me" — the hanging-post on which the Romans would soon execute him, as they had thousands before him. This would be the equivalent of John the Baptist, who was beheaded by Herod, telling his disciples and others who followed him to "take up your *guillotine and follow me."

The cross has become very popular in today's world, as hundreds of millions are wearing it around their necks and other places, and thousands of Christian churches are teaching the masses through songs and sermons to worship and bow down to the Roman cross. BLACK PEOPLE, WAKE UP!

---

*Guillotine: a machine used for beheading.

Matthew 16:13-18: "Upon This Rock . . ."

To highlight the passage, we find Yeshua asking his disciples, "Whom do men say that I the Son of man am?" The disciples began quoting what they had heard from others: "Some say you're John the Baptist: some say Elias [Elijah]; and others, Jeremias, or one of the prophets." (Apparently, in those days belief in Reincarnation was prevalent.) Yeshua then asks them the question, "But whom say ye that I am?" Peter answers, "Thou art the Christ, the Son of the living God." Yeshua gives the honor to his Father in heaven for revealing to Peter the answer. Then in verse 18, Yeshua is recorded as having said:

> *"And I say also unto thee, That thou art Peter, **and upon this rock I will build my church, and the gates of hell shall not prevail against it.**"*

The problem with Matthew 16:16 and 18 is that only in the Gospel of Matthew is the conversation between Yeshua and the disciples quoted in this way. The same occasion is recorded in the Gospels of Mark (8:29) and Luke (9:20). In Mark, Peter simply says, *"Thou art the Christ."* In Luke, Peter replies, *"Thou art the Christ of God."* Neither Mark nor Luke carry the phrases *"Son of the living God"* or *"upon this rock I will build my church."* It stands to reason that two such declarations so essential to the Christian faith would be recorded in the same way, or at least nearly so, in each of the Gospels in which they appear. *Christ* means *anointed:* Yeshua was the anointed *(Christ)* of God, and was one of the sons of God. Within the four Gospels, the word *church* appears only in Matthew: once in 16:18, and twice in 18:17; in each case it is published as a *red-letter quote* from Yeshua. *"Upon this rock I will build my church"* (16:18) and the use of *church* in 18:17 are not Yeshua's words, as he did not establish the Christian Church, neither was it even in existence during his lifetime.

John 3:16-18: Are These Really Yeshua's Words?

[16]"For God so loved the world, that he gave his only begotten Son, that whosoever believeth on him should not perish, but have everlasting life."

[17]"For God sent not his Son into the world to condemn the world; but that the world through him might be saved."

[18]"He that believeth on him is not condemned: but he that believeth not is condemned already, because he hath not believed in the name of the only begotten Son of God."

In all probability, these are the most powerful passages in the entire Greek Scriptures which set forth the Christian doctrine of Jesus as the only begotten Son of God, that exalt him as the savior of the world, and extol his name above all other names. **All three verses are in complete opposition to those eternal truths set forth by the ancient Hebrew prophets and others among the righteous; and if it does not harmonize with those revelations, we refuse to believe it, regardless of the source.**

It is dozens of passages in the Greek Scriptures like those above which have placed Yeshua in competition with the Almighty and Most High God, and have helped thrust much of the world into utter idolatry.

John 3:16: Yeshua (Jesus) was not and is not the only begotten Son of God! That is contrary to what YAH Elohim – the LORD God – has said. Many are the times in the Hebrew Scriptures when the Most High called others His sons and His daughters, in a spiritual way. In Exodus 4:22-23, the Most High said:

"And thou shalt say unto Pharoah, Thus saith the LORD, Israel is My son, even My firstborn: and I say unto thee, Let My son go, that he may serve Me: and if thou refuse to let him go, behold I will slay thy son, even thy firstborn.

In Psalm 2:6-8, **the Lord God calls David His son,** saying:

"Yet have I set My king [David] *upon My holy hill of Zion."*
I will declare the decree: the LORD hath said unto me [David],
"Thou [David] *art My son, this day have I begotten thee."*

So we see here that *Yeshua was not* God's only begotten son, but that David, king of Israel, was also the begotten son of God. In II Samuel 7:13, 14 and I Chronicles 17:11-13, **God calls Solomon His son;** and in Isaiah 43:6, the dispersed, outcast and downtrodden of Israel are rendered **the sons and daughters of God.**
This whole idea of Yeshua (Jesus) as the only begotten Son of God is based on the myth of the immaculate conception and virgin birth. (See pp. 59-64 of our *A Non-Christian's Response To Christianity.*)
Furthermore, in John 3:16, we are promised that "whoever *'believes on Jesus'* should not perish, but have everlasting life." Throughout the Hebrew Scriptures we are never commanded to put our ultimate belief and trust in flesh, but only in the Almighty and Most High God. It is said of our father Abraham, who was among the most righteous of men (in Genesis 15:6):

"And Abram [Abraham] *believed in the LORD; and He counted it to him for righteousness."*

In the event it is not clear who *the LORD* is, we now call attention to II Chronicles 20:20 (last part), the words of the righteous king Jehoshaphat to Israel:

"... Believe in the LORD your God, so shall ye be established; believe His prophets, so shall ye prosper."

Notice in the Tanakh (O.T.) that the prophets are never placed on the same level with the Almighty: the passage says, *"believe in"* the LORD your God; but it says, *"believe"* His prophets – that is, *believe their words, which are revelations from the Creator.* The Greek Scriptures, on the other hand, often place Yeshua on the level with the Most High.

In **John 3:17,** we are told that the purpose of Yeshua's

coming into the world was "that the world through him might be saved." It never has been the plan of the Most High and Almighty God to save the world through the flesh of anyone. This would be in stark opposition to what the Creator has declared through the prophet Isaiah (45:21-23, 25):

> (Vs. 21, last part)- *And there is no God else beside ME; a just God and a Saviour; there is none beside ME.* [22]*Look unto ME, and be ye saved, ALL the ends of the earth: for I am God, and there is none else.* [23]*I have sworn by Myself, the word is gone out of My mouth in righteousness, and shall not return, That unto ME every knee shall bow, every tongue shall swear.* " [25]*"In the* LORD *shall all the seed of Israel be justified, and shall glory.*"

In verses 21 and 22, we see that God Almighty is the GREAT I AM ("for I AM God"); He alone saves, and He does so, not through the death of someone's flesh and the shedding of someone's blood on a cross, but through our obedience to the word of God through His servants the prophets. Yeshua (Jesus) concurs (in John 6:63):

> *"It is the spirit that quickeneth; the flesh profiteth nothing: the WORDS that I speak unto you, they are spirit, and they are life.*"

The Most High further declares (Isaiah 40:6-8):

> [6]*". . . All flesh is grass, and all the goodliness thereof is as the flower of the field:* [7]*The grass withereth, the flower fadeth: because the spirit of the* LORD *bloweth upon it: surely the people is grass.* [8]*The grass withereth, the flower fadeth: but the word of our God shall stand for ever.*"

John 3:18 warns that if one does not believe on Jesus he "is condemned already, *because he hath not believed in the name of the only begotten Son of God.*" In the 4,000 years from Adam to Malachi there has never been a command in the Holy Hebrew Scriptures to believe in the name of anyone or anything other than the Great, the Almighty, the awe-inspiring King of the Universe. In II Chron. 20:20, righteous Jehoshaphat proclaims: *"Believe in the LORD your God . . .,"* and in innumerable other passages in the Tanakh (O.T.), the name of the Eternal One, and His name alone, is to be exalted. (See Deut. 28:58 and Prov. 18:10 as two of many examples.)

Once again, we remind the reader that whenever the Hebrew Scriptures use the term *the LORD,* never is it referring to the Christian "Lord Jesus," but the reference is always to *the LORD God Almighty,* Creator of the universe. Psalm 100:3 proclaims: *"Know ye that the LORD He is God . . ."* Nowhere in the Hebrew Scriptures or the Greek Scriptures does the Almighty God Himself ever command that we change our worship, our honor and our reverence of the Divine Being, and begin believing in, trusting in, praying to and worshipping any other being who breathes the breath of life, sleeps, cries, eats, bleeds and dies, or any other object whatsoever.

Therefore, in view of all of the above that has been expounded upon concerning John 3:16-18, we have reached the conclusion that three possibilities exist: (1) Either this is not a quotation of Yeshua; (2) that the real meaning of what he said and meant was lost in the translation; or (3) that the compilers and canonizers of the Greek Scriptures inserted John 3:16-18 themselves (and many other G.S. passages) to exalt Jesus as savior of the world and as divine. Remember, when you rule the world, as did the Greeks, Romans and Catholic Church for 700 years, you can do anything you want to do.

In John 17 There's a "Power Shift" from the Most High Almighty Creator to Yeshua

This fabricated "power shift" actually begins in Matthew 28:18, where Yeshua is recorded as having said,

"All power is given unto me in heaven and on earth,"

and carries over to the Gospel of John and elsewhere. The above passage is a matter of impossibility; the Most High Almighty Ruler of the Universe has never and will never relinquish His power. He declares in Deut. 32:39:

"See now that I, even I, am He, and <u>there is no god with Me.</u>"

In John 3:35, 5:22-23 and 13:3, and off-and-on throughout chapter 17, the writers of the Greek Scriptures make Yeshua (Jesus) equal with Almighty God. John 3:35 reads:

> *"The Father loveth the Son, <u>and hath given all things into his</u> <u>hand.</u>"* [5:22-23] *"For the Father judgeth no man, but <u>hath com-</u> <u>mitted all judgment unto the Son: That all men should honour</u> <u>the Son, even as they honour the Father</u> which hath sent him."* [13:3] *"Jesus knowing that <u>the Father had given all things into his</u> <u>hands,</u> and that he was come from God, and went to God."*

All of the above is what the writers of Matthew and John have recorded about Yeshua. (Matthew and John did not write those books; others did, within the first century after Yeshua, and affixed those disciples' names to them.) In the prayer given by Yeshua in Matthew 6:9-13, he closes by saying: *"For <u>Thine is the kingdom, and the power, and the</u> <u>glory, for ever."</u>* Would Yeshua contradict himself in the Gospel of John by saying that all power is now given unto him? If all power has been given unto Yeshua, then that would leave the Almighty God in a state of powerlessness.

John 17:2 states that *'God has given Jesus power over all flesh.'* In 17:5 it is recorded that *'Jesus existed before the world was.'*

We present as further rebuttal to the above passages, and to all others which seek to place anyone or anything equal with or above the Almighty and Most High Creator, words from the Eternal One Himself, as He speaks through the mouth of the prophet Isaiah (43:10-11):

> *"Ye are my witnesses, saith the LORD, and My servant whom I have chosen; that ye may know and believe Me, <u>and under-</u> <u>stand that I am He; before Me there was no God formed,</u> <u>neither shall any be after Me.</u>*

We feel compelled to quote a fairly lengthy passage from the prophet Isaiah which sets forth the Almightiness of the Eternal One and the perfect Unity of His existence. With the

Divine Being there is no "Twin-ity" and there is no "Trinity."
Select verses from the 40th chapter of Isaiah are among the
grandest in the entire Hebrew Holy Scriptures which set forth
the awesomeness of the Almighty's power and greatness:

ISAIAH 40:12-18; 21-23; 25-31

[12-18] "Who hath measured the waters in the hollow of his hand, and
meted out heaven with the span, and comprehended the dust of the
earth in a measure, and weighed the mountains in scales, and the hills
in a balance? Who hath directed the spirit of the LORD, or being His
counsellor hath taught Him? With whom took He counsel, and who
instructed Him, and taught Him in the path of judgment, and taught
Him knowledge, and showed to Him the way of understanding?
Behold the nations are as a drop of a bucket, and are counted as the
small dust of the balance: behold, He taketh up the isles as a very
little thing. And Lebanon is not sufficient to burn, nor the beasts
thereof sufficient for a burnt offering. All nations before Him are as
nothing, and vanity. To whom then will ye liken God? Or what
likeness will ye compare unto Him? [21-23] Have ye not known? Have ye
not heard? Hath it not been told you from the beginning? have ye not
understood from the foundations of the earth? It is He that sitteth
upon the circle of the earth, and the inhabitants thereof are as
grasshoppers; that stretcheth out the heavens as a curtain, and
spreadeth them out as a tent to dwell in: That bringest the princes to
nothing; He maketh the judges of the earth as vanity. [25-31] To whom
then will ye liken Me, or shall I be equal? saith the Holy One. Lift up
your eyes, and behold who hath created these things, that bringeth
out their host by number; He calleth them all by name by the
greatness of His might, for He is strong in power; not one faileth.
Why sayest thou, O Jacob, and speakest thou, O Israel, 'My way is
hid from the LORD, and my judgment is passed over from my God?'
Hast thou not known? hast thou not heard, that the everlasting God,
the LORD, the Creator of the ends of the earth, fainteth not, neither is
weary? there is no searching of His understanding. He giveth power
to the faint; and to them that have no might He increaseth strength.
Even the youths shall faint and be weary, and the young men shall
utterly fall: But they that wait upon the LORD shall renew their
strength; they shall mount up with wings as eagles; they shall run,
and not be weary; and they shall walk, and not faint."

By whatever name – YAHWEH, ELOHIM, HASHEM, ADONAI,
EL SHADDAI, or any of their English equivalents – the Most
High God has declared through Malachi the prophet:

*"For I am the LORD, I change not; therefore ye sons of Jacob
Jacob are not consumed"* (Mal. 3:6).

The phrase *I change not,* in Malachi 3:6, by interpretation means *"I change not from being the* LORD *God."* The same Almighty Spirit Power which brought the universe into existence untold eons ago, is the same Almighty Spirit Power which rules, governs and controls the universe today. That Power declares in the pages of Holy Scripture, through His prophets: *"My glory will I not give to another."*

"I AM THE WAY, THE TRUTH, AND THE LIFE . . ."
(John 14:1-6)

Chapter 14 of John begins with Yeshua comforting his disciples. He is not speaking to the multitude here, but only to the twelve. (The small italic line over the chapter reads, *Christ comforteth his disciples.*) He begins (in verses 1-3):

> [1] *"Let not your heart be troubled: ye believe in God, believe also in me* [2] *In my Father's house are many mansions: if it were not so I would have told you.* <u>*I go to prepare a place for you.*</u> [3] <u>*And if I go and prepare a place for you, I will come again, and receive you unto myself, that where I am there ye may be also."*</u>

Yeshua (vs. 4) says to his disciples, *"And whither I go ye know, and the way ye know."* Thomas then responds (vs. 5), *"We know not whither thou goest; and how can we know the way?"* Yeshua answers him (vs. 6), <u>*"I am the way, the truth, and the life; no man cometh unto the Father but by me."*</u>

John 14:6 (*"I am the way"*) is used worldwide by televangelists and thousands of other proselyting Christians as they make the claim that of the six billion people who now populate the earth, "not one of them can possibly come to God except through and by way of the Lord Jesus." Is John 14:6 <u>really</u> a quotation of Yeshua? Let us say for the moment that it is. Every true prophet of the Almighty and Most High God is *the way, the truth,* and *the life,* while he lives. When Moses lived, he was the way, truth and life, pointing Israel, and the mixed multitude who accompanied Israel out of Egypt, to the *written way,* the Ten Commandments, the Creator's Holy Law. And so it was with the prophets succeeding Moses.

The reason why Yeshua was able to say that he was the way, the truth and the life is due to the fact that he walked in the way (the law of the Almighty, John 15:10), taught and lived the truth, and was an example of a righteous life. Just as Yeshua stated in John 9:5, *"As long as I am in the world, I am the light of the world,"* it stands to reason that within the same context John 14:6 is intended to be understood: (that) *As long as I am in the world, "I am the way, the truth, and the life: no man cometh unto the Father, but by me."* Yeshua is no longer in the world; therefore, he is not the light of the world today, nor is he the way, the truth and the life today.

When we consider the righteousness exemplified in the lives of such men as Noah, Daniel, Job, Abraham, Moses and Hezekiah, to name a few, it can be truthfully said that each of them, in his time, was also *the way, the truth and the life.* Being "the way, truth and life" does not apply to any one individual, but to anyone and everyone walking in the commandments, statutes and judgments of the Most High.

The question most naturally to arise at this juncture of our discourse is, *Who is the way, the truth and the life today?* The answer is found is Psalm 15:2-5, and applies to anyone, anywhere, who follows the admonition of the psalmist:

> [2]*"He that walketh uprightly, and worketh righteousness, and speaketh the truth in his heart.* [3]*He that backbiteth not with his tongue, nor doeth evil to his neighbour, nor taketh up a reproach against his neighbour.* [4]*In whose eyes a vile person is contemned* [dispised]; *but he honoureth them that fear the LORD. He that sweareth to his own hurt, and changeth not.* [5]*He that putteth not out his money to usury, nor taketh reward against the innocent. He that doeth these things shall never be moved."*

We see the intent of John 14:6 directed toward the teaching and example of Yeshua, not toward his flesh and blood. He admonishes in John 6:63 that *"the flesh profiteth nothing: the words that I speak unto you, they are spirit and . . . life."*

In the italicized quote by Yeshua on page 54 (the underscored portion beginning with *"I go to prepare a place for you . . .,"* to the end of verse 3), he promises his disciples, *"I will come again . . .,"* receive them, and that he and they will be together.

According to many New Testament authorities, Yeshua (Jesus) expected some who lived during his lifetime to still be alive to *"see the Son of man coming in his kingdom."* This expectation is borne out in Yeshua's own words, from what is recorded in John 14:1-3, and in Matthew 16:27-28, which reads thusly:

> [27] *"For the Son of man shall come in the glory of his Father with his angels; and then he shall reward every man according to his works.* [28] *Verily I say unto you, There be some standing here, which shall not taste of death, till they see the Son of man coming in his kingdom."*

The writers of the Greek Scriptures record the same promise from Yeshua – the coming of his kingdom during the lifetime of those whom he addressed – in Matthew 24:29,30,33,34; Mark 9:1 and Luke 9:27:

Matthew 24:29,30,33,34

> [24] *"Immediately after the tribulation of those days shall the sun be darkened, and the moon shall not give her light, and the stars shall fall from heaven, and the powers of the heavens shall be shaken:* [30] *And then shall appear the sign of the Son of man in heaven: and then shall all the tribes of the earth mourn, and they shall see the Son of man coming in the clouds of heaven with power and great glory.* [33] *So likewise ye, when ye shall see all these things, know that it is near, even at the doors.* [34] *Verily I say unto you, This generation shall not pass, till all these things be fulfilled."*

Mark 9:1

> *"And he said unto them, Verily I say unto you, That there be some of them that stand here, which shall not taste of death, till they have seen the kingdom of God come with power."*

Luke 9:27

"But I tell you of a truth, there be some standing here, which shall not taste of death, till they see the kingdom of God."

The above passages from three of the Gospels all declare that the kingdom of God would come before the death of some of the generation to whom Yeshua was speaking. The more we examine the prophecy, the more we question whether they are the words of Yeshua. More than 2,000 years have passed since the supposed utterance of the above passages, and the generation to whom he spoke has also long since passed. To date the Son of man has not "come in the clouds of heaven with power and great glory" to usher in the kingdom of God, as promised in the Gospels.

The *secong coming of Christ* is one of the paramount beliefs of the Christian Church. We, however, do not ascribe to this tenet, not only because the promises from the Gospels and the writings of the Apostle Paul on the subject have failed, but for a myriad of practical reasons, as well.

The number of Christians globally has reached 2.1 billion, which is nearly one-third of the world's population. Those of us who follow the Hebrew Israelite way given to ancient Israel by Moses and the prophets, and have accepted the Almighty and Most High Creator as our Saviour and Redeemer, are not awed by the enormity of those Christian numbers. But rather, this author concurs with Yeshua's words from Matthew 7:13-14, which show that the majority is not always right:

[13]*"Enter ye in at the strait gate: for wide is the gate, and broad is the way, that leadeth to destruction, and many there be which go in thereat:* [14]*Because strait is the gate, and narrow is the way, which leadeth unto life, and few there be that find it."*

We are encouraged even moreso by the words of the Most High Himself from the prophecy of Isaiah 2:1-4 (Heb. Vers.):

[1]*"The word that Isaiah the son of Amoz saw concerning Judah and Jerusalem.* [2]*And it shall come to pass in the end of*

days, that the mountain of the LORD's house shall be established as the top of the mountains, and shall be exalted above the hills; and all nations shall flow unto it. ³*And many peoples shall go and say: 'Come ye, and let us go up to the mountain of the LORD, to the house of the God of Jacob; and He will teach us of His ways, and we will walk in His paths.' For out of Zion shall go forth the law, and the word of the LORD from Jerusalem.* ⁴*And He shall judge between the nations, and shall decide for many peoples; And they shall beat their swords into plowshares, and their spears into pruninghooks; nation shall not lift up sword against nation, neither shall they learn war any more."* (See Micah 4:1-3.)

What a prophecy! Destined to be fulfilled in the Messianic Age, according to Holy Scripture.

The topic of this chapter, *"DID YESHUA REALLY SAY THAT?"*, is almost inexhaustible; for we could continue on endlessly throughout the pages of the Gospels pointing out discrepancy after discrepancy. Many such inconsistencies not appearing in this publication are addressed rigidly in our other books.

The conclusion of the whole matter is this: Christianity has built an entire religion completely centered around a human being whom they named *Jesus Christ* many years after his death. Christianity, in conjunction with the Greco-Roman Empire, or vice versa, has compiled and canonized a new scripture and has named it *THE NEW TESTAMENT OF OUR LORD AND SAVIOUR JESUS CHRIST*. In this compilation they have falsified many of the facts about this young prophet, whose real name was YESHUA BEN YOSEF.

This Hebrew Israelite rabbi was just thirty years old when he announced his public ministry on a Sabbath in the synagogue at Nazareth. For the next three years he went on to do great works for humanity and to teach Divine truths from the Law, the Prophets, and the Writings. During his lifetime he often upbraided those who "taught for doctrines the commandments and tradition of men" (Matt. 15:3-6; vs. 9).

Warning: Be not deceived by the slavemaster's religion!

CHAPTER 5

How Christianity 'Stole' Jesus and Adopted Him As Its Founder and Saviour-God

THE MANNER OF HIS CONCEPTION AND BIRTH has been falsified; the date of his birth is off by far; his racial identity has been changed from Black African-Asian to Caucasian, and his name has gone from the Hebrew *Yeshua ben Yosef* (Joshua son of Joseph) to the Latin/Greek *Iésous Christos* (Jesus Christ). But it doesn't stop there: His way of life and nationality – Hebrew Israelite – has been snuffed out and replaced by the adoption of him as the founder of Christianity, of which the Roman Catholic Church is the head.

None of the above took place during his lifetime, however, but gradually, within the first three centuries after his death. To elaborate on the five points mentioned in the paragraph above, we find that the immaculate conception and virgin birth story had its origin in ancient Egyptian and Babylonian mythology, and more recently in Greek and Roman mythology, when Alexander the Great invaded Egypt in 332 B.C.E. and carried all of its wisdom, along with its mythological system, to Greece. The date of Christmas was set at the Nicene Council of 325 C.E. (A.D.). The rulers of Yeshua's day – the Greeks and Romans – determined that he would look like them and their pagan gods and goddesses, so they whitened Yeshua's image. As we have said in previous writings, Yeshua never heard the name *Jesus* or the title *Christ*. If he were across the street right now and you shouted out, *"Jesus! Jesus Christ!"*, he wouldn't even respond; but he would answer to the name *Yeshua ben Yosef.* (The name *Jesus/Iésous* borders on *Zeus,* chief of the Olympian Greek gods, and with the Roman god Jupiter.) And lastly, why would Yeshua, after 33 years of being a practicing Israelite, with a three-year ministry as a rabbi, change his entire belief system and become the founder of Christianity, a religion based on the worship of a man – himself? Cannot you see the thievery and deception involved in this entire picture?

Not only have the Greeks, Romans and Roman Catholic Church fashioned their Jesus into a god and the founder of the Christian Church, but they have named his head apostle, Simon Peter, as the Church's first pope. In seeking to authenticate these fabrications as truths, they have taken steps to have them placed into the Encyclopædia Britannica and other major resource publications, where they have appeared now for hundreds of years.

It is difficult to ascertain just when the Church as an institution really began. We have already established on page 47, last paragraph, that the word *church* in the Gospels appears only in Matthew (once in 16:18 and twice in 18:17), and that its usage is attributed to Yeshua, with which we disagree. Mark, Luke, and John are silent on the word *church,* even though Mark and Luke give an account of the same event recorded in Matthew 16:13-18.

After Matthew, the next mention of *church* does not appear until Acts 2:47, where it is stated:

"And the Lord added to the church daily such as should be saved."

We can say with utmost certainty that the *church as an edifice* or *building* had not then been established, because in the verse before Acts 2:47 (verse 46), it tells how *"the apostles continued daily in the temple . . ."* Little by little in the Book of Acts there seems to be a drifting away from the teaching and doctrines set forth by Yeshua, and, as recorded in Acts 2:42, the move is toward the embracing of a new way:

*"And they continued stedfastly in **the apostles' doctrine** and fellowship, and in breaking bread, and in prayers."*

This *apostles' doctrine* was not according to the teaching of the Torah and the Prophets, which were taught by Yeshua, but was a doctrine which glorified Jesus, embracing him as *Lord and Saviour* (with capitals *L* and *S*), as had been done, to a lesser degree, throughout the four Gospels.

The exaltation of the name of *Jesus* began in the Gospels and continued in the Book of Acts. Apostle Peter reportedly preaches the crucifixion and resurrection of Yeshua in Acts 4:10, and says of him in verse 12:

*"Neither is there salvation in any other: **for there is none other name under heaven given among men, whereby we must be saved.**"*

But throughout the Hebrew Scriptures we are taught over and over again by the Almighty and Most High Creator and by His holy prophets, priests and kings to place our ultimate trust only in the Great and Mighty King of the Universe, to hallow only His name, and that salvation is only in Him..

In Acts chapter 9 Saul, who is called Paul, begins his rise to prominence, telling of his vision and conversion on the Damascus road, where it is said that Jesus shined a light brighter than the sun (Acts 26:13), and spoke to Saul from heaven. (There are three accounts of this incident in the Book of Acts, and each contradicts the other: Acts 9:7, 22:9, and 26:13, 14.)

Acts 9:13-15 has Jesus speaking from heaven to Ananias in a vision, telling him that this Saul (Paul) *"is a chosen vessel unto me, **to bear my name** [the name of Jesus, that is] **before the Gentiles, and kings, and the children of Israel.**"* The Greek Scriptures continue place after place to exalt the name of Jesus above the name of the Most High. The writers thereof made secondary the exaltation of the King of the Universe, which the prophets of the Hebrew Scriptures extolled and worshipped. A few passages from the Hebrew Scriptures follow, showing forth the greatness and majesty of the Name of the Omnipotent Divine Being and Eternal One, who always was, who is, and who shall forever be:

Exodus 9:14-16
(The words of the Most High to Pharoah, through Moses)

[14] *"For I will this time send all My plagues upon thy person, and upon thy servants, and upon thy people; that thou mayest know that THERE IS NONE LIKE ME IN ALL THE EARTH.*
[15] *Surely now I could have put forth My hand, and smitten thee and thy people with pestilence, and thou would have been cut off from the earth.* [16] *But in very deed for this cause have I made thee to stand, to show thee My power, and that MY NAME MAY BE DECLARED THROUGHOUT ALL THE EARTH."*

Psalm 46:10

"Be still, and know that I AM GOD; I WILL BE EXALTED AMONG THE HEATHEN, I WILL BE EXALTED IN THE EARTH."

Malachi 1:11 & 14

[11] *"For from the rising of the sun even unto the going down of the same MY NAME SHALL BE GREAT AMONG THE GENTILES; and in every place incense shall be offered unto MY NAME, and a pure offering: for MY NAME SHALL BE GREAT AMONG THE HEATHEN, saith the LORD of hosts."*
[14] *"But cursed be the deceiver, who hath in his flock a male, and voweth, and sacrificeth unto the LORD a corrupt thing: for I AM A GREAT KING, saith the LORD of hosts, and MY NAME IS DREADFUL AMONG THE HEATHEN."*

The idea of Jesus' name being *"borne among the Gentiles, kings, and the children of Israel"* (Acts 9:15) is contrary to the teaching of the prophets. From the beginning of Genesis to the end of Malachi is approximately 4,000 years. During that time span the Almighty and Most High Being was both constant and worshipped. There were about 397 years between Malachi and Matthew, and since the dawn of the C.E. (A.D.) period, the ruling powers have sought to introduce to the world a new god – Jesus – despite all that has been declared by the Almighty Himself, the biblical prophets, and Yeshua.

The Greek Scriptures (New Testament) repeatedly "plays tricks" with the prophecies of the Hebrew Scriptures, deceiving the masses into believing that the conception, birth, ministry, death, resurrection and ascension of Yeshua are foretold in the Prophets and the Psalms. There are more than 100 such passages in the Gospels and in the epistles of Paul, yet not one of them is a fulfillment of the prophecies referenced. **In Matthew 12:18-21, there is a scripture they have extracted from Isaiah 42:1-4, which Christians claim is a prophecy relating to Yeshua, though it is not. We suggest that you follow this observation very closely, as it is just one example of what the Greek Scriptures have done to deceive those unknowledgeable of the scriptures.** (For an unabridged account of over 100 prophecies from the Tanakh (O.T.) and how it is proved conclusively that they do not relate to Yeshua, we suggest that you obtain copies of two of our books entitled *"The Deceiving of the Black Race"* and *"A Non-Christian's Response To Christianity."*)

Let us now compare the two passages mentioned above, Matthew 12:18-21 and Isaiah 42:1-4:

Matthew 12:18-21

[18] *"Behold My servant, whom I have chosen; My beloved, in whom My soul is well pleased: I will put My spirit upon him, and he shall show judgment to the Gentiles.* [19]*He shall not strive, nor cry; neither shall any man hear his voice in the streets.* [20]*A bruised reed shall he not break, and smoking flax shall he not quench, till he send forth judgment unto victory.* [21]And in his name shall the Gentiles trust."*

Isaiah 42:1-4 (King James Version)

[2] *"Behold My servant, whom I uphold; Mine elect, in whom My soul delighteth; I have put My spirit upon him, he shall bring forth judgment to the Gentiles.* [2]*He shall not cry, nor lift up, nor cause his voice to be heard in the street.* [3]*A bruised reed shall he not break, and the smoking flax shall he not quench; he shall bring forth judgment unto truth.* [4]*He shall not fail nor be discouraged, till he has set judgment in the earth; and the isles shall wait for his law [teaching, HS]."*

First of all, Isaiah chapter 42 is not a prophecy relating to Yeshua or any other individual, but it speaks of Israel as a people. Although the phrases in verse 1 say, *Behold My servant* and *My elect,* and are in the singular, if you read Isaiah 43:1,10,11; 44:1,2,21; 45:4, and other related scriptures from the Prophets, you will see that it is Israel who is "God's servant" and "God's elect." (See pages 68-70 in our book *A Non-Christian's Response To Christianity.*)

We have examined Isaiah 42:1-4 from five different versions of the Bible, and in not one of them does the verse appear which is recorded in Matthew 12:21: *"And in his name shall the Gentiles trust."* This verse in Matthew has been inserted by the compilers of the Greek Scriptures with the intent to deceive people into believing that God has foretold from Isaiah 42 that the Gentiles will trust in the name of Yeshua (Jesus). This is just one instance among hundreds. The Creator has ordained that we place our ultimate trust only in Him, and that we exalt and magnify His name only.

Because of the Greek, Roman, and Catholic Church influence in the world over the last 2,000 years, approximately 2.1 billion Christians – Gentile and non-Gentile alike – are trusting in the name of Jesus, with hundreds of millions praying to him and even worshipping and bowing down to images through paintings and statues of him. The point to be made here is that there is no Divine authority anywhere in the Hebrew Scriptures to support any of these idolatrous practices.

Statistics on African American Christians

Millions of indigenous Africans and millions who are of African ancestry in the Americas and throughout the world now embrace Christianity. C. Eric Lincoln, in his book, THE BLACK CHURCH IN AMERICA, states that there are 38.4 million African Americans in the United States, and that 86 per cent of that number are Christians. This translates into more than 33 million African Americans who now profess Christianity, and just slightly over five million who do not. These statistics are just for the United States, not to mention Africa, and the rest of the western hemisphere where the slaves were deposited. And just how did we of African ancestry globally, whose forefathers and -mothers were brought to this hemisphere in slave ships from 1517 onward, come to be Christians? Through the slavemaster, of course, by way of brute force.

How Pertinent the Upcoming Point!

I am fully aware that the questions and statements which we are about to set forth have been mentioned in one of our former publications. But they are of such utmost importance that we find it necessary to repeat them, in the event you missed them the first time around:

Do you think for a moment that a just, Almighty Creator, whom the Scriptures bespeak as "righteous in all His ways and holy in all His works," would allow the wicked, cruel, abominable slavemaster – who raped your mother, daughter and sister, and who castrated, burned and lynched your father, brother and son for 350 years -- to give you the TRUE Religion? (The word *religion* is not in the Hebrew Scriptures; it is of Greek origin.) **The Most High did not allow the Egyptians to give ancient Israel the true way of life, after their 430 years' sojourn in Egypt. But rather, he raised up Moshé (Moses), who taught them commandments, statutes, judgments and ordinances.** "ANYONE WHO WON'T TREAT YOU RIGHT, WON'T TEACH YOU RIGHT!" YES, THAT'S RIGHT: CHRISTIANITY IS THE SLAVE-MASTER'S RELIGION!! **And there's no getting around it!**

All this is part of the thievery by Christianity mentioned in this chapter's main heading on page 59. Not only did they steal Yeshua, but they also stole between 50 million and 100 million people out of Africa between 1517 and 1865, and thrust them into rigorous slavery for 348 years.

Was Yeshua Sent to the Whole World?

In his own words, the answer is "No." Matthew 10:5-6 states that Yeshua told his disciples to go only to the Israelites:

> [5] *"These twelve Yeshua sent forth, and commanded them, saying, Go not into the way of the Gentiles, and into any city of the Samaritans enter ye not:* [6]*But go rather to the lost sheep of the house of Israel."*

The above passage, however, contradicts what is recorded that Yeshua said in Matt. 28:19 and in Mark 16:15, where it is said that he told his disciples,

> [28:19] *"Go ye therefore, and teach all nations, baptizing them in the name of the Father, and of the Son, and of the Holy Ghost . . ."* [Mk. 16:15] *"Go ye into all the world, and preach the gospel to every creature."*

An even greater contradiction appears in the stories recorded in Matt. 15:21-28 and in Mark 7:24-30. It is the same event, but the nationality of the woman in the story changes from *Canaanite* (in Matthew) to *Greek, Syro-phenician* (in Mark). It is pertinent that you engage in this study and discover the blatant inconsistency that exists. We will first quote from Matt. 15:21-28:

> *"Then Yeshua went thence, and departed into the coasts of Tyre and Sidon. And, behold, a woman of Canaan came out of the same coasts, and cried unto him, saying, 'Have mercy on me, O Lord, thou son of David; my daughter is grievously vexed with a devil.' But he answered her not a word. And his disciples came and besought him, saying, 'Send her away; for she crieth after us.' But he answered and said, 'I am not sent but unto the lost sheep of the house of Israel.' Then she came and worshipped him, saying, 'Lord, help me.' But he answered and said, 'It is not meet to take the children's bread, and to cast it to dogs.' And she said, 'Truth, Lord: yet the dogs eat of the crumbs which fall from the masters' table.' Then Yeshua answered and said unto her, 'O woman, great is thy faith: be it unto thee even as thou wilt.' And her daughter was made whole from that very hour."*

We will now quote the exact same incident from Mark 7:24-30; notice the major discrepancy, which will be underlined:

"And from thence he [Yeshua] *arose, and went into the borders of Tyre and Sidon, and entered into an house, and would have no man know it: but he could not be hid. For a certain woman, whose young daughter had an unclean spirit, heard of him, and came and fell at his feet:* <u>*The woman was a Greek, a Syro-phenician by nation;*</u> *and she besought him that he would cast forth the devil out of her daughter. But Yeshua said unto her, 'Let the children first be filled: for it is not meet to take the children's bread, and to cast it unto the dogs.' And she answered and said unto him, 'Yes, Lord: yet the dogs under the table eat of the children's crumbs.' And he said unto her, 'For this saying go thy way; the devil is gone out of thy daughter.' "*

Was the woman in the story a Canaanite, a Black woman descended from Ham (Gen. 10:6 and 15)? Or was she a Greek, a White woman descended from Japheth (Gen. 10:2), who migrated into the Caucasus regions and formed the nations of Europe? There is a mix-up somewhere in the two Gospels carrying the story.

We have undeniable proof that the woman in the story was a Greek, Syro-phenician by nation, as Mark records. <u>Yeshua would have never refused to help a woman of Canaan who was calling after him, for YESHUA HAD A CANAANITE DISCIPLE. Have not you read of Simon the Canaanite in Matt. 10:4? Yes, he was one of the twelve. The man Canaan was the son of Ham and the grandson of Noah – all Black African-Asian people!</u>

Furthermore, in the story Yeshua calls the Greek woman "a dog" in Mark 7:27, saying, *". . . it is not meet to take the children's bread, and to cast it unto the dogs."* The implication is strong that this was his human feeling towards the Gentiles. Yeshua often spoke unkindly of the Gentiles during his ministry, probably because of the way they had invaded

Jerusalem/Judea and oppressed the Israelites before and during his day. Other passages in which the Gentiles are spoken of in disfavor by Yeshua include: Matt. 6:31,32; 10:6,18; 20:19; Mark 10:33; Luke 18:32; 21:24. The Gentiles against whom he spoke were the Greeks and the Romans. Notice that Yeshua had no Gentile disciples. Although the names of Mark and Luke are listed as Gospel writers, they were not disciples of Yeshua. The names of the twelve appear in Matt. 10:2-4: Simon Peter, Andrew, James, John, Philip, Bartholomew, Thomas, Matthew, James the son of Alphæus, Lebæus (same as Thaddæus), Simon the Canaanite, and Judas Iscariot. Mark, and the Greek Caucasian Luke are not among them..

Lastly on the subject of *the Canannite*, we direct your attention to Ezekiel 16:1-3:

> [1] *"Again, the word of the LORD came unto me, saying,* [2]*Son of man, cause Jerusalem to know her abominations,* [3]*And say, Thus saith the Lord GOD unto Jerusalem;* <u>*Thy birth and thy nativity is of the land of Canaan; thy father was an Amorite, and thy mother a Hittite.*</u>*"*

From this, we see that the Israelites, whose holy city was Jerusalem, had their beginning in the land of Canaan. The Amorites and the Hittites were a part of the Canaanite family of nations. (See Gen. 10:15-18.)

So the conclusion of the whole matter, within the context of the subject at hand, is that Yeshua was not sent to the whole world, but to Israel for his day. The Greeks, Romans, and the Roman Catholic Church 'stole' him and made him their savior-god and king. More than 2,000 years following his death, round-the-clock Christian radio and TV stations and churches proclaim that Yeshua is coming soon. The Almighty and Most High Creator Himself has not proclaimed in either Scripture anything about the second coming of Yeshua, but rather, the GREAT I AM <u>has</u> declared, *"Look unto <u>Me</u>, and be ye saved, all the ends of the earth: for I am God, and there is none else beside Me!"* (Isa. 45:22.)

CHAPTER 6

The Best of the Greek Scriptures (N.T.)

ALTHOUGH THE GREEK SCRIPTURES HAVE BORROWED 484 quotations from the Hebrew Scriptures to make up the compilation of its 27 books, there is still a good deal of independent beauty in the Christians' sacred book.

Yeshua's famous *Sermon On the Mount* includes the whole of Matthew chapters 5, 6 and 7, in which there is much beautiful teaching. Verses 3-12 contain the *Beattitudes,* which, in our opinion, are the most comforting portion of the *Sermon.* Let us now rehearse them:

> [3]*"Blessed are the poor* [humble] *in spirit: for theirs is the kingdom of heaven.* [4]*Blessed are they that mourn: for they shall be comforted.* [5]*Blessed are the meek: for they shall inherit the earth.* [6]*Blessed are they which do hunger and thirst after righteousness: for they shall be filled.* [7]*Blessed are the merciful: for they shall obtain mercy.* [8]*Blessed are the pure in heart: for they shall see God.* [9]*Blessed are the peacemakers: for they shall be called the children of God.* [10]*Blessed are they which are persecuted for righteousness' sake: for theirs is the kingdom of heaven.* [11]*Blessed are ye, when men shall revile you, and persecute you, and shall say all manner of evil against you falsely, for my sake.* [12]*Rejoice, and be exceeding glad: for great is your reward in heaven: for so persecuted they the prophets which were before you."*

Certainly, if the world would seek to live according to the above teaching, especially verses 3-9, peace and happiness would prevail. For to be "humble in spirit," "comforted when mourning," "to be meek," "to hunger and thrist after righteousness," and "to be a peacemaker" are the main ingredients for a happy life and for global tranquility.

Other noteworthy passages in the *Sermon On the Mount* include Matt. 5:14, where Yeshua makes it clear that not only was he the light of the world, but he also encourages his followers, saying, *"Ye are the light of the world, a city that is set on a hill."* He further admonishes them (in 5:16) to *"Let your light so shine before men, that they may see your good works, and glorify your Father which is in heaven."*

In 5:17-19, Yeshua makes it abundantly clear that he did not come to destroy the law or the prophets, but to fulfill. He reinforces the endurance of God's Holy Law, the importance of keeping it, and the dangers of breaking the least of the commandments and teaching others to do so.

In Matt. 6:9-13 is the pattern for prayer. It is known as *The Lord's Prayer;* we prefer to call it *The Disciples' Prayer,* as it was given to them at the request of one of them (Luke 11:1). Since the Almighty God is our LORD, and He has no need to pray because He is the Most High, hence *The Disciples' Prayer* rather than *The Lord's Prayer.* Notice in the prayer that Yeshua's (Jesus') name does not appear at all. The petitions are totally directed to the Heavenly Father, His name alone is hallowed, and the coming of His kingdom and the doing of His will are also emphasized. Verses 9-10 contain *the exaltation;* verses 11-12 and a portion of verse 13, *the petition,* and the balance of verse 13, *the benediction,* where Yeshua once again glorifies the Creator:

"For Thine is the kingdom, and the power, and the glory, for ever. Amen.

In Matthew 7:15, Yeshua warns to *"Beware of false prophets, which come to you in sheep's clothing, but inwardly they are ravening wolves."* In verse 21 the implication is that merely screaming "Jesus, Jesus, Jesus!" will not guarantee entrance into the kingdom of heaven, *"but he that doeth the will of my Father which is in heaven."*

As we continue with *The Best of the Greek Scriptures* (N.T.), we say without reservation that Yeshua's many parables are truly gems of wisdom. Just what is a parable? According to Webster's Collegiate Dictionary, a parable is defined as follows: *A comparison; specifically, a short ficticious narrative from which a moral or spiritual truth is drawn.* In A COMPLETE ANALYSIS OF THE BIBLE, a parable is described as: *A method of teaching through pictures of human life.* This source goes on to say that this method was much employed in ancient times, and striking instances occur in the Old Testament, notably Nathan's parable of the ewe-lamb by which David was made his own judge (II Sam. 12:1-7).

Of the 28 parables set forth by Yeshua, we find the most interesting and enjoyable to be *The Sower* (Mt.. 13:4-8), *The Prodigal Son* (Lu. 15:11:32), and *The Rich Man and Lazarus* (Lu. 16:19-31). The latter receives the greater nod and is also the most amusing, in our estimation. We shall review it as recorded, and then comment thereon:

"There was a certain rich man, which was clothed in purple and fine linen, and fared sumptuously every day: and there was a certain beggar named Lazarus, which was laid at his gate, full of sores, and desiring to be fed with the crumbs which fell from the rich man's table: moreover the dogs came and licked his sores. And it came to pass, that the beggar died, and was carried by the angels into Abraham's bosom: the rich man also died, and was buried; and in hell he lift up his eyes, being in torments, and seeth Abraham afar off, and Lazarus in his bosom. And he cried and said, Father Abraham, have mercy on me, and send Lazarus, that he may dip the tip of his finger in water, and cool my tongue; for I am tormented in this flame. But Abraham said, Son, remember that thou in thy lifetime receivedst thy good things, and likewise Lazarus evil things: but now he is comforted, and thou art tormented. And beside all this, between us and you there is a great gulf fixed: so that they which would pass from hence to you cannot; neither can they pass to us, that would come from thence. Then he said, I pray thee therefore, father,

*that thou wouldest send him to my father's house: for I have
five brethren; that he may testify unto them, lest they also
come into this place of torment. Abraham saith unto him,
They have Moses and the prophets; let them hear them. And
he said, Nay, father Abraham: but if one went unto them from
the dead, they will repent. And he said unto him, If they hear
not Moses and the prophets, neither will they be persuaded,
though one rose from the dead."*

In the parable, the Rich Man, unlike Lazarus, remains
nameless. However, during my late teenage years, somewhere
along the way I learned that Christian theologians had given
him the name of DIVEES. There is a verse in an old Negro
Spiritual about the parable of the Rich Man and Lazarus that
lends support to the name DIVEES, and it is as follows:

*Poor old Lazarus, poor as I, don't you see!
Poor old Lazarus, poor as I, don't you see!
Poor old Lazarus, poor as I, when he died he had a home
    on high;
I've got a home in that Rock, don't you see!*

*Rich man Divees lived so well, don't you see!
Rich man Divees lived so well, don't you see!
Rich man Divees lived so well, when he died he had a home
    in hell;
I've got a home in that Rock, don't you see!*

There are several lessons in the parable of The Rich Man
and Lazarus. One is, that we should be considerate and very
concerned about the poor and others who are less fortunate
than we, and if not, there are consequences either in this life or
in the Judgment.

The Torah and the Prophets command consideration for
the poor, requiring of those who farm not to glean every
corner of their fields, but to leave some for the poor. The
Most High proclaims through the prophet Isaiah (58:6,7) that
a real fast is more than abstaining from food and drink and
being sad-faced, but also must include the following if it is to
be accepted by the Creator:

[58:6] *"Is not this the fast that I have chosen? To loose the bands of wickedness, to undo the heavy burdens, and to let the oppressed go free, and that ye break every yoke?* [7]*Is it not to deal thy bread to the hungry, and that thou bring the poor that are cast out to thy house? When thou seest the naked, that thou cover him; and that thou hide not thyself from thine own flesh?"*

Another lesson to be learned from the parable is that of not embracing a "spooky" religion, whereby someone has to rise from the dead and warn you to be righteous, lest you end up in hell. One of the other lessons emphasized in the story is that if you read the Hebrew Scriptures and obey them, wherein are contained the teaching of "Moses and the Prophets," you will not find yourself in the predicament of the Rich Man.

Among the many righteous patriarchs, prophets and kings mentioned throughout the Tanakh (O.T.) that Yeshua could have chosen to embosom Lazarus, he chose the only one of whom the Almighty had spoken thusly: *"Abraham, My friend for ever."*

The Rich Man probably thought that he could get over on Abraham by addressing him as "father," and throwing into the mix his concern for his five brethren. Abraham, who tenderly called him "son," was not about to fall for the Rich Man's 'jive,' neither was he going to disturb Lazarus' comfortable position in his bosom to send him on a mission to the Rich Man's non-repentant brethren. Why should he? They all knew right from wrong, but had chosen the wrong over the right. The most lofty reason for doing that which is just and right, anyway, is *"because it is right to do that which is just and right,"* and not in hope of heaven or in fear of hell!

OTHER WONDERFUL PASSAGES
WITHIN THE GREEK SCRIPTURES

There are 14 epistles of Apostle Paul, from the book of Romans to the book of Hebrews. The total number of chapters contained in all his epistles are exactly 100. Among these writings are found what we have determined to be two masterpieces. One is I Corinthians chapter 13, which Christian biblical historians have called *the Love Chapter,* and the other is Hebrews chapter 11, *the Faith Chapter.* Whereas the King James Version (KJV) of the Bible carries the word *charity* as the topic of I Corinthians 13, most of the versions published within the last forty or so years renders the topical word as *love.*

As two examples, we will quote just three verses of the chapter in question from the GOOD NEWS BIBLE, published by the American Bible Society of New York (1966/1976), and from the NEW WORLD TRANSLATION OF THE HOLY SCRIPTURES, published by the Watch Tower Bible & Tract Society of New York, Inc. (1961, Jehovah's Witnesses). Following these quotations, we will render the chapter in its entirety from the KJV to show the excellency of this passage from the Greek Scriptures.

From the Good News Bible

[1]*"I may be able to speak the languages of men and even of angels, but if I have no love, my speech is no more than a noisy gong or a clanging bell.* [2]*I may have the gift of inspired preaching; I may have all knowledge and understand all secrets; I may have all the faith needed to remove mountains – but if I have no love, I am nothing.* [3]*I may give away everything I have, and even give up my body to be burned – but if I have no love, this does me no good."*

From the New World Translation (Jehovah's Witnesses)

[1]*"If I speak in the tongues of men and of angels, but do not have love, I have become a sounding piece of brass or a clashing cymbal.* [2]*And if I have the gift of prophesying and am acquainted with all the sacred secrets and all knowledge, and if I have all the faith so as to transplant mountains, but do not have love, I am nothing.* [3]*And if I give all my belongings to feed others, and if I hand over my body, that I may boast, but do not have love, I am not profited at all."*

Before presenting the entire chapter from the KJV, a

marked peculiarity of the passage should be noted: How odd that within the entire chapter of I Corinthians 13, with its 13 verses, no mention or inference whatsoever is made of God, Lord, Jesus or Christ. Of the 14 epistles attributed to Paul, which embrace 100 chapters, this is the only one in which there is no inclusion of God or Jesus/Christ. In fact, many of his epistles carry what to us is an over-abundance of *Jesus* and *Christ* references, and to a lesser degree the mention of God. To document this, our research reveals that within the 14 epistles *Christ* and *Jesus* combine for a total of 926 times, whereas *God* appears 627 times. *Lord* is used 293 times; ninety-two percent of the time it applies to "the Lord Jesus," not to YAH ELOHIM – the LORD God Almighty.

What is written above, however, does not negate the fact that the 13th chapter of I Corinthians is one of Paul's two thought-provoking masterpieces. This chapter is not in disagreement with what is taught in the Law and the Prophets.

I Corinthians Chapter 13 (KJV)

"Though I speak with the tongues of men and of angels, and have not charity, I am become as sounding brass, or a tinkling cymbal. And though I have the gift of prophecy, and understand all mysteries, and all knowledge; and though I have all faith, so that I could remove mountains, and have not charity, I am nothing. And though i bestow all my goods to feed the poor, and though I give my body to be burned, and have not charity, it profiteth me nothing. Charity suffereth long, and is kind; charity envieth not; charity vaunteth not itself, is not puffed up, doth not behave itself unseemly, seeketh not her own, is not easily provoked, thinketh no evil; rejoiceth not in iniquity, but rejoiceth in the truth; beareth all things, believeth all things, hopeth all thinhs, endureth all things. Charity never faileth: but whether there be prophecies, they shall fail; whether there be tongues, they shall cease; whether there be knowledge, it shall vanish away. For we know in part, and we prophesy in part. But when that which is perfect is come, then that which is in part shall be done away. When I was a child, I spake as a child, I understood as a child, I thought as a

child: but when I became a man, I put away childish things. For now we see through a glass, darkly; but then face to face: now I know in part; but then shall I know even as also I am known. And now abideth faith, hope, charity, these three; but the greatest of these is charity."

But is *charity* really *love?* Usually when we think of charity, giving comes to mind. However, we do not think that giving alone makes one charitable, because people give for many different reasons. Some give to receive recognition and praise, while others may give out of fear of being criticized if they do not give, or because everyone else in the group is giving, and they would rather not be among the odd ones.

If *charity* is *love,* then *charity* may be defined as "giving out of love and concern." For "you can give without loving, but you cannot love without giving."

In the 11th chapter of Hebrews – *the Faith chapter* – Paul calls a roll of 18 stalwart, faithful men and women of the Hebrew Scriptures. We highly applaud this chapter of his *epistle, which gives a brief synopsis of what many who lived in those times endured for the sake of righteousness.

We consider the writer's definition of *Faith,* in verse 1, to be most eloquently appropriate:

"Now faith is the †substance of things hoped for, the evidence of things not seen."

Furthermore, the writer of the chapter is very generous with his use of the word *God,* and gives glory and honor to Him who often chooses to deliver some in this life, and chooses not to deliver others, but to assign them to an even better and everlasting deliverance.

Hebrews chapter 11 contains forty verses. Its beauty and grandeur far outweigh its lack of brevity. We will not allow

----
*An *epistle* is a letter. It is pronounced e-PIS-sul; the *t* is silent.
†The word *substance* in Hebrews 11:1, above, is translated as *assurance.*

the improper use of the word *Christ* in verse 26 to cloud our assessment of this masterful text, despite the fact that the verse makes Christ retroactive to the time of Moses, saying:

> *"Moses esteemed the reproach of <u>Christ</u> greater riches than the treasures of Egypt . . ."*

Although this is done over and over again in the Greek Scriptures, it is both untrue and unfounded. Hebrews 11, nevertheless, is still a gem of a chapter, and we have decided to render it in its entirety:

> **"Now faith is the substance of things hoped for, the evidence of things not seen. For by it the elders obtained a good report. Through faith we understand that the worlds were framed by the word of God, so that things which are seen were not made of things which do appear. By faith Abel offered unto God a more excellent sacrifice than Cain, by which he obtained witness that he was righteous, God testifying of his gifts: and by it he being dead yet speaketh. By faith Enoch was translated that he should not see death; and was not found, because God had translated him: for before his translation he had this testimony, that he pleased God. But without faith it is impossible to please Him; for he that cometh to God must believe that He is, and that He is a rewarder of them that diligently seek Him. By faith Noah, being warned of God of things not seen as yet, moved with fear, prepared an ark to the saving of his house; by the which he condemned the world, and became heir of the righteousness which is by faith. By faith Abraham, when he was called to go out into a place which he should after receive for an inheritance, obeyed; and he went out not knowing whither he went. By faith he sojourned in the land of promise, as in a strange country, dwelling in tabernacles with Isaac and Jacob, the heirs with him of the same promise: for he looked for a city which hath foundations, whose builder and maker is God. Through faith also Sara herself received strength to conceive seed, and was delivered of a child when she was past age, because she judged Him faithful who had promised. Therefore sprang there even of one, and him as good as dead, as many as the stars of the sky in multitude, and as the sand which is by the sea shore innumerable. These all died in faith, not having received the promises, but having seen them afar off, and were persuaded of them, and embraced them, and confessed that they were strangers and pilgrims on the earth. For they that say such things declare plainly that they seek a country. And truly, if they had been mindful of that country from which they came out, they might have had opportunity to have returned. But now they desire a better country, that is an heavenly; wherefore God is not ashamed to be called their**

God: for He hath prepared for them a city. **By faith Abraham, when he was tried, offered up Isaac; and he that had received the promises offered up his only begotten son, of whom it was said, 'That in Isaac shall thy seed be called': accounting that God was able to raise him up, even from the dead; from whence also he received him in a figure. By faith Isaac blessed Jacob and Esau concerning things to come. By faith Jacob, when he was a-dying, blessed both the sons of Joseph, and worshipped, leaning upon the top of his staff. By faith Joseph, when he died, made mention of the departing of the children of Israel; and gave commandment concerning his bones. By faith Moses, when he was born, was hid three months of his parents, because they saw he was a proper child; and they were not afraid of the king's commandment. By faith Moses, when he was come to years, refused to be called the son of Pharoah's daughter; choosing rather to suffer affliction with the people of God, than to enjoy the pleasures of sin for a season; esteeming the reproach of *Christ* greater riches than the treasures in Egypt: for he had respect unto the recompense of the reward. By faith he forsook Egypt, not fearing the wrath of the king: for he endured as seeing Him who is invisible. Through faith he kept the passover, and the sprinkling of blood, lest He that destroyed the firstborn should touch them. By faith they passed through the Red Sea as by dry land: which the Egyptians assaying to do were drowned. By faith the walls of Jericho fell down, after they were compassed about seven days. By faith the harlot Rahab perished not with them that believed not, when she had received the spies with peace. And what shall I more say? For time would fail me to tell of Gideon, and of Barak, and of Samson, and of Jephthæ; of David also, and Samuel, and of the prophets: who through faith subdued kingdoms, wrought righteousness, obtained promises, stopped the mouths of lions, quenched the violence of fire, escaped the edge of the sword, out of weakness were made strong, waxed valient in fight, turned to flight the armies of the aliens. Women received their dead raised to life again: and others were tortured, not accepting deliverance: that they might obtain a better resurrection: and others had trial of cruel mockings and scourgings, yea, moreover of bonds and imprisonment: they were stoned, they were sawn asunder, were tempted, were slain with the sword: they wandered about in sheepskins and goatskins; being destitute, afflicted, tormented; (of whom the world was not worthy:) they wandered in deserts, and in mountains, and in dens and caves in the earth. And these all, having obtained a good report through faith, received not the promise: God having provided some better thing for us, that they without us should not be made perfect."**

Select Passages From the Book of James, Brother of Yeshua

We conclude this section of the book, *The Best of the Greek Scriptures,* by highlighting writings from the BOOK OF JAMES. His Hebrew name was *Yaacov* (pron. YÄ-a-cōv), and when translated from Hebrew to English, is equivalent to *Jacob.* He was one of Yeshua's brothers (Matt. 13:55; Mark 6:3). This is a different James from the two mentioned as Yeshua's disciples in Matt. 10:2,3 (James, son of Zebedee, and James, son of Alphæus). His book is dated at the year 60, and is addressed to the twelve tribes scattered abroad (1:1).

We are particularly fond of these writings because they express in various places the sentiments of the many eternal truths found in the Hebrew Scriptures. In this segment we will quote a few of the passages from THE GENERAL EPISTLE OF JAMES which are not contradictory to, but are in harmony with, the teachings of Moses and the Prophets. The writer upholds the Law of God, and refers to it in one place as *the perfect law of liberty,* and in another as *the law of liberty.*

James 1:22-25: *"But be ye doers of the word, and not hearers only, deceiving your own selves. For if any be a hearer of the word, and not a doer, he is like unto a man beholding his natural face in a glass: For he beholdeth himself, and goeth his way, and straightway forgetteth what manner of man he was. But whoso looketh into the perfect law of liberty, and continueth therein, he being not a forgetful hearer, but a doer of the work, this man shall be blessed in his deed."*

In his endeavor to continue his sanction of the Ten Commandments, James (in 2:10-12) makes the following claim:

"For whosoever shall keep the whole law, and yet offend in one point, he is guilty of all. For He that said, 'Do not commit adultery,' said also, 'Do not kill.' Now if thou commit no adultery, yet if thou kill, thou art become a transgressor of the law. So speak ye, and so do, as they that shall be judged by the law of liberty."

Also in chapter two there is a very edifying admonition on *Faith* and *Works,* in verses 14-18, wherein it is stated that "faith without works is dead." We find it necessary to review this most interesting passage:

> (2:14-18) "What doth it profit, my brethren, though a man say he hath faith, and have not works? Can faith save him? If a brother or sister be naked, and destitute of daily food, and one of you say unto them, 'Depart in peace, be ye warmed and filled'; notwithstanding ye give them not those things that are needful to the body; what doth it profit? Even so faith, if it hath not works, is dead, being alone. Yea, a man may say, 'Thou hath faith,' and I have works: shew me thy faith without thy works, and I will shew thee my faith by my works."

In verse 20 the importance of works is emphasized again: *"But wilt thou know, O vain man, that faith without works is dead."* The rest of the chapter (verses 21-26) goes on to tell of the good works of Abraham and Rahab, how that they, too, were justified by works:

> [21]"Was not Abraham our father justified by works, when he had offered Isaac his son upon the altar? [22]Seest thou how faith wrought with his works, and by works was faith made perfect? [23]And the scripture was fulfilled which saith, 'Abraham believed God, and it was imputed unto him for righteousness; and he was called the Friend of God.' [24]Ye see then how that by works a man is justified, and not by faith only. [25]Likewise also was not Rahab the harlot justified by works, when she had received the messengers, and had sent them out another way? [26]For as the body without the spirit is dead, so faith without works is dead also."

As we have seen, the Book of James places great emphasis on Works and less of an emphasis on Faith alone. Apostle Paul does just the opposite. He says that Abraham and that long roll of stalwarts listed in Hebrews chapter 11 were justified by Faith. Yet James' discourse in his second chapter places works as foremost and faith as secondary. We have determined this as THE JAMES-PAUL DEBATE, and consider the argument presented by Yaacov (James) to have the edge.

This concludes our dissertation on *The Best of the Greek Scriptures.*

CHAPTER 7

If Yeshua Was Not/Is Not the Saviour of the World, Who, Then, Is?

THE ANSWER TO THE LEAD QUESTION is a relatively easy one, and will be forthcoming from the pages of the Hebrew Holy Scriptures. We have contended in all of our books and lectures – and we will continue to contend, and prove – that Yeshua ben Yosef (Jesus son of Joseph) is not the saviour of the world and did not die for the sins of the world. Nowhere in the Gospels, which carry the life and works of Yeshua, did _he_ ever make such a claim. There is, however, a sparse mention of him as the saviour by one or two others writing of him in the Gospels. The Book of Acts of the Apostles goes full speed ahead in promoting the doctrine of Yeshua as the savior of the world, and this idea is also vehemently pursued in all of Apostle Paul's epistles to the Gentiles. In Acts 4:12 Peter reportedly makes the following declaration about Yeshua (Jesus) and his name:

> "Neither is there salvation in any other: for there is no other name under heaven given among men, whereby we must be saved."

We do not understand how Peter could have uttered such a statement, after having spent three years under his master, Yeshua, who was a scholar of the Torah and the Prophets, where only the name of the Almighty and Most High God is magnified and exalted.

The word _save_ has several synonyms, three of which are _redeem, salvage/salvation, safeguard._ Before we go into the volume of the book – the Holy Scriptures – and show there-

81

from just who is the ultimate and Eternal Saviour of mankind, allow us to direct your attention to one of the missing links in the understanding of Yeshua's message, and that is, that he often spoke of himself in the present tense and for the time in which he lived. A prime example is his frequent use of the phrase "I am": viz., *I am the way," "I am the true vine," "I am the living bread which came down from heaven," "I am the light of the world," "I am the door of the sheep,"* etc. The phrase *I am* is present tense; not past tense, not future tense. When he lived he was all of the above (except that Yeshua did not literally "come down from heaven").

There are several instances in the Hebrew Scriptures where individuals used *I am* to describe their then present situations. In Judges 17:9, one man declares:

"*I am a Levite of Beth-lehem-judah, and I go to sojourn where I may find a place."*

In I Kings 13:18, one prophet says unto another:

"*I am a prophet also as thou art . . ."*

Nehemiah (in 6:3) says to his adversaries while the walls of Jerusalem were being rebuilt:

"*I am doing a great work, so that I cannot come down . . ."*

In Jonah 1.9, the prophet declares,

"*I am an Hebrew, and I fear the God of heaven."*

The prophet Micah the Morasthite (in 3:8) makes the following declaration:

"*But truly I am full of power by the spirit of the LORD, and of judgment, and of might . . ."*

The above are just a few of the passages in the Hebrew Scriptures where *I am* is used by those speaking in the present tense at the time. Surely we would not expect the above passages to still hold true today now that we are, in most cases, more than 2,500 years removed from those times. Yeshua was who he was when he lived on earth, but since his cessation the many "*I am's*" used by him were for then, not for now. Just as he made it clear in John 9:5 that, *"As long as I am in the world, I am the light of the world,"* logic and common sense dictate that it would hold just as true that *"I am the way," "I am the true vine," "I am the door of the sheep,"* etc., would also be in effect only *"as long as I am in the world."*

WHO, THEN, IS THE SAVIOR?

Among the more than 2.1 billion Christians worldwide, their Lord and saviour is Jesus Christ. Yet, most of the world's more than six billion people are not Christians, and do not ascribe to the doctrine of Jesus Christ as their Lord and saviour. This translates into more than four billion people globally who are not adherents of Christianity. Among these are one billion-plus Muslims; nearly 760 million Hindus; 340 million Buddhists, and Hebrew Israelites worldwide and European Jews, who combine for an approximate total of 40-plus million. All of these, and many others, such as Chinese Folk Religionists, Sikhs, Confucians, Baha'is, Jains, and Shintoists, do not accept Jesus Christ as their Lord and saviour.

Hundreds of Christian televangelists and other ministers, as well as an untold number of Christian lay members, have condemned to an eternal burning hell all who do not accept Yeshua (Jesus) as their personal saviour and who have not been washed in his blood. This is not the teaching of Yeshua, but of Paul, who has caused more people to be misled than any other contributor to the scriptures.

The Almighty and Most High God of the Holy Scriptures declares place after place that He alone is the LORD, and beside Him there is no Saviour. David in II Samuel 22:3 proclaims the Almighty as his Saviour, and in Psalm 106:21, the writer recounts the conduct of ancient Israel under Moses, and states that God was their Saviour. II Samuel 22:3 and Psalm 106:21 read as follows:

> *"The God of my rock; in Him will I trust: He is my shield, and the horn of my salvation, my high tower, and my refuge, my*

Saviour; Thou savest me from violence."

"They forgat God their Saviour, who had done great things in Egypt . . ."

And now for the scriptures where the Almighty and Most High God Himself says that He is the Saviour, not only of Israel, but the Saviour of the world:

Isa. 43:3,11 - [3]*"For I am the LORD thy God, the Holy One of Israel, thy Saviour . . ." *[11]*"I, even I, am the LORD; and beside Me there is no saviour."*

Isa. 45:15,21 – [15]*"Verily Thou art a God that hidest Thyself, O God of Israel, the Saviour." *[21]*"Tell ye, and bring them near; yea, let them take counsel together; who hath declared this from ancient time? Who hath told it from that time? Have not I the LORD? And there is no God else beside Me; a just God and a Saviour; there is none beside Me."*

Isa. 45:22,23 - [22]***"Look unto Me, and be ye saved, all the ends of the earth: for I am God, and there is none else." ***[23]***"I have sworn by Myself, the word is gone out of My mouth in rightousness, and shall not return, That unto Me every knee shall bow, every tongue shall swear."***

Isa. 49:26 - *"And I will feed them that oppress thee with their own flesh; and they shall be drunken with their own blood, as with sweet wine: **and all flesh shall know that I the LORD am thy Saviour and thy Redeemer, the mighty One of Jacob."***

Isa. 60:16 - *"Thou shalt also suck the milk of the Gentiles, and shalt suck the breast of kings: and thou shalt know that I the LORD am thy Saviour and thy Redeemer, the mighty One of Jacob."*

Isa. 63:8 - *"For He said, Surely they are My people, children that will not lie: **so He was their Saviour.***

Jer. 14:8 - ***"O the Hope of Israel, the Saviour thereof in time of trouble,** why shouldest Thou be as a stranger in the land, and as a wayfaring man that turneth aside to tarry for a night?"*

Hosea 13:4 - *"Yet I am the LORD thy God from the land of Egypt, **and thou shalt know no god but Me: for there is no Saviour beside Me."***

What we have not presented thus far is the definition of the word *saviour*. According to Webster's Collegiate Dictionary, a *saviour* is: *one who saves or delivers*. This suggests that someone can be your saviour who saves you from a burning building or delivers you from the jaws of a ferocious beast. But within the context of this discussion, we are speaking of the one and only Spiritual Saviour and Redeemer who forgives sin and pardons iniquity, as it is written in the prophet Isaiah:

> *"Let the wicked forsake his way, and the unrighteous man his thoughts: and let him return unto the LORD, and He will have mercy upon him; and unto our God, for He will abundantly pardon."*

The scriptures presented on page 84 pertaining to the Most High as Saviour present undeniable proof that the God of Abraham, the God of Isaac, and the God of Jacob – and He alone – is the Saviour of the world. He is the Creator of the ends of the earth, and there is no searching of His understanding, for His ways are past finding out.

It has already been established (on page 81) that the word *salvation* is a derivative of *save*. Aside from the many references in the Hebrew Scriptures (O.T.) which testify of the Eternal One as the one and only Saviour, there are likewise nearly 120 passages within the writings of the Hebrew prophets which proclaim that *SALVATION* IS ONLY OF THE ALMIGHTY AND MOST HIGH YAH ELOHIM – THE LORD GOD! "MY GLORY," says the King of kings, "WILL I NOT GIVE TO ANOTHER, NEITHER MY PRAISE TO GRAVEN IMAGES!"

We make no apologies for the hard line which we take against the Christian pastors and teachers and those of any other religious persuasion who place another being in the stead of the Most High God, the Creator of the ends of the earth. The Almighty Sovereign of the universe wants His people to return unto Him and worship Him in spirit and in truth. The very idea of tens of millions of people of African ancestry in the western hemisphere – most of whom are the distant descendants of the ancient Israelites – worshipping and praying to Yeshua instead of to the Giver of Life, the very Life of the universe, is unconscionable. It was Yeshua who taught: *"Thou shalt worship the LORD thy God, and Him only shalt thou serve"* (Matt. 4:10), and likewise taught that we pray, *"Our Father which art in heaven, Hallowed be Thy name"* (Matt. 6:9). (The word *hallowed* means *to make holy; to consecrate.* Notice that in Matt. 6:9 (KJV) the word *Hallowed* is capitalized, even though it is not the beginning of a sentence nor is it the beginning of a quotation.)

Institutionalized slavery has scattered and destroyed the people of the Most High God. It is our mission, through the grace and power of the Almighty, to bring back to Him the lost sheep of the house of Israel. (See Eze. 34:11-12 and Matt. 10:5-6.) We implore every person of African ancestry to read and study the 28th chapter of Deuteronomy to discover what the Creator said would happen to us as a people if we failed to worship, serve and obey Him. **The Almighty and Most High God, and He alone, is our only Hope. We have tried everything else for nearly 500 years, and it has failed.** (See page 40 of our book entitled *"THE DECEIVING OF THE BLACK RACE,"* for a complete discussion and commentary on Deuteronomy chapter 28, and discover who you really are.)

Do you want your sins forgiven? Do you want to be redeemed? It is as simple as placing yourself at the mercy of the Most High God, through prayer and supplication.

Isaiah 1:18: *"Come now, and let us reason together, saith the LORD: though your sins be as scarlet, they shall be as white as snow; though they be red like crimson, they shall be as wool."*

Couple that scripture with Isaiah 44:22, where the forgiving and merciful Creator decrees:

"I have blotted out as a thick cloud thy transgressions, and, as a cloud, thy sins: return unto Me; for I have redeemed thee."

It is not necessary to pray to or go through Yeshua or any

other person in order to pour out your soul unto your Maker. As we return, just for a moment, to a portion of the Disciples' Prayer recorded in Matt. 6:12, we are taught by Yeshua to petition the Almighty, and Him alone, to *"Forgive us our debts* [our sins], *as we forgive our debtors* [those who sin against us]. Nothing is said in the Prayer about going through or praying to the author of the invocation. .

There are 24-hour-a-day Christian radio and television stations and channels which scream that "JESUS IS THE ANSWER!" and "JESUS IS LORD!" from the rising of the sun on one day until the rising of the sun on another – deceiving the nations. It is not Yeshua who is the answer, but it is the Commandments of God which he taught that is the answer. Despite the false teaching which for centuries has been forced upon people of African ancestry, the word has gone forth out of the mouth of the Almighty and Most High God, in Psalm 46:10: *"Be still, and know that I AM God: I will be exalted among the heathen, I will be exalted in the earth."* True Israel and all others who will join with him, promise to hold fast to the words of the Lawgiver Moses in Deuteronomy 32:3, whereby we will *". . . Proclaim* [publish] *the name of the LORD:* [and] *ascribe greatness unto our God."*

"My people are destroyed for lack of knowledge: because thou hast rejected knowledge, I will also reject thee, that thou shalt be no priest to me: seeing thou hast forgotten the law of thy God, I will also forget thy children." (Hosea 4:6.)

THE GREAT CONCLUSION: Isaiah 43:10:
"Ye are My witnesses, saith the LORD, and My servant [Israel] *whom I have chosen: that ye may know and believe Me, and understand that I am He: before Me there was no God formed, neither shall there be after Me."*

CHAPTER 8

Is Christ 'Our Passover', As Paul Claims?

His flim-flam epistles to the Gentiles blatantly and often contradict the O.T. Prophets & Yeshua

THE BIBLICAL ACCOUNT OF THE EXODUS of the children of Israel from Egyptian bondage more than 3,000 years ago is universally known. The central figure of the Exodus was Moses the Lawgiver, who was chosen by the Almighty and Most High God as Israel's deliverer.

PASSOVER (Heb. Pésach; pron. **pā'**-sök), therefore, is the memorial of that glorious event, and the remembrance of it is so great that the Most High has declared in Torah (Ex. 12:14):

> *"And this day shall be unto you for a memorial; and ye shall keep it a feast to the LORD throughout your generations; ye shall keep it a feast by an ordinance for ever."*

Furthermore, to accentuate its importance, of the 39 books of which the Hebrew Scriptures is composed, 30 of them record Israel's deliverance from Egyptian servitude in some way – in the Torah, in the Prophets, and in the Writings.

From the birth of Moses in ca. 1571 B.C.E. to the birth of Yeshua was just short of 1600 years, and even then we find him at age 12 going up to Jerusalem with his parents to observe the Feast of the Passover (Luke 2:41,42):

> [41]*Now his parents went to Jerusalem every year at the feast of the passover.* [42]*And when he was twelve years old, they went up to the passover after the custom of the feast."*

88

All four Gospels – Matthew, Mark, Luke, and John – carry the account of Yeshua's last Passover. Matthew, in 26:17-18:

[17]*"Now the first day of the feast of unleavened bread the disciples came to Jesus, saying unto him, Where wilt thou that we prepare for thee to <u>eat the passover</u>?* [18]*And he said, Go into the city to such a man, and say unto him, The Master saith, My time is at hand; I will keep the passover at thy house with my disciples."*

The writer of the Gospel of Mark (in 14:12-15) records the same event – Yeshua's last Passover – in this way:

[12]*"And the first day of unleavened bread, when <u>they killed the passover,</u> his disciples said unto him, Where wilt thou that we go and prepare that thou mayest <u>eat the passover</u>?* [13] *And he sendeth forth two of his disciples, and saith unto them, Go ye into the city, and there shall meet you a man bearing a pitcher of water; follow him.* [14]*And wheresoever he shall go in, say ye to the goodman of the house, The Master saith, Where is the guestchamber, where <u>I shall eat the passover</u> with my disciples?* [15]*And he will shew you a large upper room furnished and prepared: there make ready for us."*

In the Gospel of Luke (22:7-11) preparation for Yeshua's last Passover is carried thusly:

[7]*"Then came the day of unleavened bread, when <u>the passover must be killed.</u>* [8]*And he sent Peter and John, saying, Go and prepare us the passover, <u>that we may eat.</u>* [9]*And they said unto him, Where wilt thou that we prepare?* [10]*And he said unto them, Behold, when ye are entered into the city, there shall a man meet you, bearing a pitcher of water; follow him into the house where he entereth in.* [11]*And ye shall say unto the goodman of the house, Where is the guestchamber, where <u>I shall eat the passover with my disciples?"</u>*

The Gospel of John makes no mention of any preparations for Yeshua's last Passover as did the other Gospel writers. In chapter 13 supper has already ended when the story begins. John, too, is the only Gospel which records the washing of the disciples' feet by their master. Feet-washing was an old Hebraic custom and can be traced to the Hebrew Scriptures.

The first five verses of John 13 give us an idea of the humility possessed by Yeshua, who taught that "he that is greatest among you, let him be the servant." This was the example being set by him when he kneeled and washed and wiped the feet of the twelve:

> [1] *"Now before the feast of the passover, when Jesus knew that his hour was come that he should depart out of this world unto the Father, having loved his own which were in the world, he loved them unto the end.* [2]*And supper being ended, the devil having now put into the heart of Judas Iscariot . . . to betray him;* [3]*Jesus knowing that the Father had given all things into his hands, and that he was come from God, and went to God;* [4]*He riseth from supper, and laid aside his garments; and took a towel, and girded himself.* [5]*After that he poureth water into a basin, and began to wash the disciples' feet, and to wipe them with the towel wherewith he was girded."*

Is Yeshua 'Our Passover'?

Paul reminds us of how the late Dr. Martin Luther King, Jr., likened some people to a grasshopper: "When a grasshopper is on green grass, it's green; when it's on brown grass, it's brown; when it's on yellow grass, it's yellow." Paul made the statement: *"I am made all things to all men, that I might by all means save some."* **You just cannot be all things to all men; if you try to do so, you will end up being neither hot nor cold, but lukewarm.**

Paul states in I Corinthians 5:7 the following:

> *"Purge out therefore the old leaven, that ye may be a new lump, as ye are unleavened. For even Christ our passover is sacrificed for us."*

Nowhere in the teaching of Yeshua did he ever say that he is 'our passover'. We have taken the time to quote all those passages from the Gospels which give an account of Yeshua's last passover, and in each passage we have underlined those portions where Yeshua himself has stated that he would *"eat this passover with my disciples."* If

Yeshua is the passover, then when he says in Matthew 26:17, for instance, that he will *'eat the passover with his disciples,'* and when Mark records that on the first day of unleavened bread, *'they killed the passover,'* it would be absurd to believe that he would *'eat himself,'* or that the verses were speaking of him when they say that the *'passover was killed on the first day of unleavened bread.'* No, Yeshua is neither *'our passover'* nor 'the passover,' but rather, he observed the Passover by partaking of the unleavened bread, the Paschal lamb and the wine. These things he had done from his youth, and which Israelites had been observing since the time of Moses. It was easy for Paul to sell his watered-down beliefs to the pagan Gentiles of Greece and Rome. What did they know about the will of the Most High God? They had been worshipping idols for centuries, until the advent of Paul.

The truth of the matter is this, and it cannot be denied: PAUL (or whoever wrote those 14 epistles from Romans through Hebrews) WAS A JESUS CHRIST FREAK! All of the epistles attributed to Paul total exactly 100 chapters. There is only one chapter that does not contain the name of Jesus in some form (Jesus, Christ, Jesus Christ, or Christ Jesus), and that is the 13th chapter of I Corinthians. All told, *Jesus* and *Christ* combine for a total of 926 times in the epistles, and *God* appears 627 times. *Lord* is used 293 times, but ninety-two percent of the time it applies to "the Lord Jesus," not to the LORD God Almighty.

There are so, so many untruths and inaccuracies in those 14 epistles. Let's examine a few more of them:

ROMANS 3:3 - *"For this man* [Christ Jesus] *was counted worthy of more glory than Moses, inasmuch as he who hath builded the house hath more honour than the house."*

By what authority does Paul say that Yeshua was counted worthy of more glory than Moses? Certainly, he did not speak through Divine Revelation. Yeshua would have never placed himself above the Lawgiver, the one who, through the power and might of the Almighty, laid the very foundation for holiness, righteousness, morality, ethics and business for all Israel – past, present and future – and for much of the world. It is statements like, "Christ Jesus was counted worthy of more glory than Moses," which continue to fan the fires of discord between Christians and those of the Judaic persuasion.

Paul comes across unfounded again in Ephesians 3:9 and in Philippians 2:6, where he over-speaks Yeshua's position:

> Eph. 3:9 - *"And to make all men see what is the fellowship of the mystery, which from the beginning of the world hath been hid in God, **who created all things by Jesus Christ"**: . . .-*

> Phil. 2:6 - *"Who [Christ Jesus], being in the form of God, **thought it not robbery to be equal with God"**: . . .*

Ephesians 3:9 contradicts what is recorded in Isaiah 44:24, where the Almighty Himself declares: <u>*"I am the LORD that maketh all things; that stretchest forth the heavens alone; that spreadest abroad the earth by Myself."*</u>

Philippians 2:6 is completely out of control, as Paul places Yeshua (Jesus) "equal with God." The Divine Being speaks in Isaiah 40:18, 25: *"To whom then will ye liken God? or what likeness will ye compare unto Him?* In verse 25 the Creator asks: *"To whom then will ye liken Me, or <u>shall I be equal?</u> saith the Holy One."* In John 14:28 Yeshua says, *". . . For <u>the Father is greater than I.</u>"* If God is <u>greater</u> than Yeshua, how, then, can Yeshua be <u>equal</u> with God?

We could continue almost endlessly pointing out in passage after passage in the 14 epistles of Paul the many times in which he not only contradicts, misquotes and misconstrues what is recorded in the Hebrew Scriptures, but also how he ofttimes contradicts himself, as well. Charles Potter, in his book *THE STORY OF RELIGION* (Simon & Schuster, 1929) states that Paul would have been a perfect specimen for a psychiatrist's couch, and questions whether Paul was abnormal or a genius. There is one thing we must admit, and that is that the Apostle to the Gentiles was an intellectual and certainly had a way with words. This is possibly the reason why Festus, the Roman governor of Judea, said to him after his eloquent speech before King Agrippa, "Thou art beside thyself; much learning doth make thee mad."

On the First Chapter of Hebrews

To close out this chapter, we ask that you please indulge our thoughts and our rebuttals on Hebrews chapter 1.

According to the biblical arrangement, HEBREWS is the last of Paul's epistles. It is simply called in one Bible *THE EPISTLE TO THE HEBREWS;* and in another *THE EPISTLE OF PAUL THE APOSTLE TO THE HEBREWS.*

Yet, as we review this epistle we see very little therein to which the ancient Hebrews from the time of Abraham through the time of Yeshua could really relate. In the first five verses – **Hebrews 1:1-5** – the writer debases what the Most High has revealed to the prophets of the Hebrew Scriptures, and exalts Yeshua (Jesus) above all that ever was, that is, and that shall ever be. Paul (or whoever wrote HEBREWS) has destroyed the original meaning of what has been referenced in Hebrews chapter 1 from the Hebrew Scriptures (O.T.). This is done over and over again in the overwhelming majority of his epistles. Let us now review the chapter and its incongruities:

> [1] *"GOD, who at *sundry times and in *divers manners spake in time past unto the fathers by the prophets, [2]Hath in these last days spoken unto us by His Son, whom He hath appointed heir of all things, by whom also He made the worlds";*

Rebuttal, verses 1 & 2: The implication seems to be that 'although God spoke to the fathers through the prophets, I, Paul, say to ignore those Divine Revelations, and believe now only in Jesus.' We see nowhere in scripture where the Most

---

*Both *sundry* and *divers* mean *various; different.*

High God Himself or any of the prophets ever said that Yeshua or anyone else has been "appointed heir of all things," or that the Creator "made the worlds by Yeshua." The out-of-context biblical reference used by Paul to try to prove that Yeshua was "appointed heir of all things" by the Creator, is Psalm 2:8: *"Ask of Me, and I shall give thee the heathen for thine inheritance, and the uttermost parts of the earth for thy possession."* First off, the Most High in Psalm 2 was speaking to and about king David and the people of Israel, not to or about Yeshua. Read all of Psalm 2, and you will see. (We have acddressed this Psalm in its entirety on pages 115-117 in our book *A NON-CHRISTIAN'S RESPONSE TO CHRISTIANITY.*) Psalm 2:8 is not saying that anyone, not even David, has been "appointed heir of all things." Paul has falsely applied many, many scriptures from the Tanakh (O.T.) to bolster the idea to the Gentiles and to the Christian world that Yeshua was their Lord and Saviour. Hundreds of millions of people to this day believe all of the rhetoric spoken by Paul. (See our commentaries on page 92 on Ephesians 3:9 and Philippians 2:6.)

In **Heb. 1:5** Paul once again wrests away the true application of Psalm 2:7 and II Samuel 7:14:

> Heb. 1:5 - *"For unto which of the angels said He* [God] *at any time, Thou art my Son, this day have I begotten thee?' And again, I will be to him a Father, and he shall be to me a Son?"*

Rebuttal, verse 5: Paul should have been ashamed of himself to have deceived the Gentiles of his day, and billions more since, into believing that the host of passages he has used from the Hebrew Scriptures were prophecies relating to Yeshua. The first portion of Hebrews 1:5 *(Thou art my Son, this day have I begotten thee")* **are the words of the Most High to king David,** from Psalm 2:7; the latter portion of the verse in Hebrews 1:5 *("I will be to him a Father, and he shall be to me a Son")* **is also the promise of the Almighty through the prophet Nathan to David concerning his son Solomon,** from II Samuel 7:14. Paul used only a <u>portion</u> of what is recorded in II Samuel 7:14; we will now quote it in its entirety:

II Sam. 7:14 - *"I will be his father, and he shall be My son. If he commits iniquity, I will chasen him with the rod of men, and with the stripes of the children of men . . ."*

We invite you to read II Samuel 7:12-17 and plainly see that these verses were the promises to David concerning his son Solomon, who was to succeed him.

There is yet another reason of great import which validates that II Samuel 7:14 foretells of Solomon, and that is the following:

The verse states, *"If he commits iniquity, I* [God] *will chasten him with the rod of men . . ."* Christianity contends that Yeshua was perfect from birth to death, never sinned and could not possiby commit any iniquity. If the verse is a reference to Yeshua, and if he was perfect and never sinned, why would the verse say, *"If he commits iniquity . . .?"*

Heb. 1:6 is deceptive and leads those unknowledgeable of the scriptures to believe that another being other than the Most High Creator is to be worshipped:

Heb. 1:6 - *"And again, when he* [God] *bringeth the first begotten* [Jesus] *into the world, he* [God] *saith, And let all the angels of God worship him."*

Rebuttal, verse 6: Absolutely nowhere within the pages of the Hebrew Scriptures (O.T.) or the Greek Scriptures (N.T.) does the Almighty and Most High God Himself ever command men or angels to worship any other being beside Him.

In **Heb. 1:8,** the writer thereof has God Almighty calling Jesus *"God"*:

Heb. 1:8 - *"But unto the Son* [Jesus] *he saith, Thy throne, O God, is for ever and ever: a sceptre of righteousness is the sceptre of thy kingdom."*

Rebuttal, verse 8: This verse is taken from Psalm 45:6 in the King James Version (KJV). But is Hebrews 1:8 directed to Yeshua, or has it been misquoted with the intent to mislead? If you read Psalm 45:6 in the KJV, it tells of David declaring that God's throne is forever, and that His sceptre is the right sceptre. If, on the other hand, you read Psalm 46:7-18 from the Hebrew Version (the most authentic one), it has an altogether different meaning, for it speaks of <u>David,</u> his throne and sceptre, as king of Israel, and a portion of the greatness of his reign. For those who do not have a copy of the Holy Scriptures in their possession, we will quote Psalm 45:7-18 from that version to show the differences between it and the KJV:

A PSALM OF THE SONS OF KORAH FOR THE KING

"Thy throne <u>given of God</u> is for ever and ever; a sceptre of equity is the sceptre of thy kingdom. Thou hast loved righteousness, and hated wickedness; therefore God, thy God, hath anointed thee with the oil of gladness above thy fellows. Myrrh, and aloes, and cassia are all thy garments; out of ivory palaces stringed instruments have made thee glad. Kings' daughters are among thy favourites; at thy right hand doth stand the queen in gold of Ophir. 'Hearken, O daughter, and consider, and incline thine ear; forget also thine own people, and thy father's house; so shall the king's desire thy beauty; for he is thy lord; and do homage unto him. And, O daughter of Tyre, the richest of the people shall entreat thy favour with a gift.' All glorious is the king's daughter within the palace; her raiment is of chequer work inwrought with gold. She shall be led unto the king on richly woven stuff; the virgins her companions in her train being brought unto thee. They shall be led with gladness and rejoicing; they shall enter into the king's palace. Instead of thy fathers shall be thy sons, whom thou shalt make princes in all the land. I [God] will make thy name to be remembered in all generations; therefore shall the people praise thee for ever and ever."

With all that we have written on the Epistle to the Hebrews, we haven't even gotten through the first chapter. It would take another complete book for us to go epistle by epistle and point out all the inaccuracies contained in those 14 letters to the Gentiles.

Chapter Summarization

Paul, in I Corinthians 5:7, calls 'Christ [Jesus] our passover,' although nowhere is it stated by Yeshua or the Gospel writers that he is. This, therefore, is Paul's totally unfounded creation. We see where Yeshua made a pilgrimage to Jerusalem with his parents to observe the passover at age twelve, and he 'ate' the passover with his disciples before his death.

~~~~

Paul is the only one in either scripture – the Hebrew or the Greek – to compare the glory and worthiness of one prophet to another, as he declares in Romans 3:3 that *"This man [Christ Jesus] was counted worthy of more glory than Moses."* We find this to be untrue and unacceptable.

~~~~

From the near-4,400-year period – the beginning of the Adamic Age to the birth of Yeshua – those who wrote of those times never suggested the existence of a co-Creator of the heavens and the earth, as did Paul in Ephesians 3:9, Philippians 2:6 and elsewhere. The writers of the Hebrew Scriptures always expounded within the realm of the four opening words of Genesis 1:1: *"In the beginning GOD . . ."*

~~~~

From that portion of the first chapter of Hebrews which we did cover, we find that Paul, in Hebrews 1:1, places the teaching of Yeshua above those of the prophets, and states that God made the worlds by His Son [Jesus]. He takes the words which the Most High spoke concerning David and Solomon (in Psa. 2:7 and II Sam. 7:14) and applies them to Yeshua. In Heb. 1:6, the writer says that when God brought the first begotten [Yeshua] into the world, that He said, 'Let the angels of God worship him.' There is no command anywhere in scripture from the Almighty Creator to worship any being but Him.

~~~~

Yeshua inserted within his parable of the Rich Man and Lazarus (p. 71-72), that the Rich Man's five sinful brethren *"have Moses and the prophets: let them hear them. If they hear not Moses and the prophets, neither will they be persuaded, though one rose from the dead."*

"MOSES AND THE PROPHETS" IS STILL THE WAY TO THE KNOWLEDGE AND WILL OF THE MOST HIGH!

CHAPTER 9

Why the Term *'So-called'* in Reference to Old & New Testaments?

WHEN SOMETHING IS REFERRED TO AS "OLD," often what comes to mind is that it is outdated and has been replaced by something "new," and in many instances, by something "better."

> The etymology and definition of the word *testament,* according to Webster's collegiate dictionary, are as follows: **testament,** *n.* [L. *testamentum* (fr. *testari* to be a witness, fr. *testis* a witness); in ref. to the Bible, translating Gr. *diathēkē* a last will, a covenant.] 1. *Bib.* A solemn covenant: **a** [caps. with *Old* and *New.*] One of two general divisions of the Scriptures. See BIBLE. **b** [cap.] Colloquially, the New Testament. (Def. **2** applies to *Law.*)

The terms *Old Testament* and *New Testament* are really misnomers, for nowhere within the confines of either division of the Bible do we see such references; hence our employment of the word *'So-called.'*

We see from the definition above that the foremost meaning of *testament* is *covenant.* So what is really meant by *Old Testament* in today's world is *Old Covenant,* and the average Christian is quick to respond thusly when you mention the Ten Commandments: "O that's the old covenant and the old Mosaic Law; we are no longer under the law, but under the new covenant and under grace."

When the Almighty God through the prophet Jeremiah (in 31:31) uses *new covenant,* He definitely is not referring to what is commonly called the New Testament – that compilation of the Greek Scriptures from Matthew to Revelation – but rather to the Sinaitic Covenant, the Ten Commandments. (For a complete, in-depth analysis and exegesis on Jeremiah 31:31-34, see pages 88-92 of our book entitled *THE DECEIVING OF THE BLACK RACE.*) Neither is Matthew 26:28 referring to *The New Testament books* when it states *"This is my blood of the new testament."* We repeat: There is nothing within the text of either the Hebrew Scriptures or the Greek Scriptures designating them as *The Old Testament* and *The New Testament.*

When Yeshua speaks of the ancient sacred writings, there is documentation that he refers to them as *the Scriptures,* or *the Law,* or *the Prophets,* or *the Psalms,* but never as the Old Testament.

Here is what Paul, the apostle to the Gentiles, has to say about the *new covenant* of Jeremiah 31:31-34:

From Hebrews 8:13 - ***"In that He saith, A new covenant, He hath made the first old. Now that which decayeth and waxeth old is ready to vanish away."***

To get the full picture of what Paul is saying about the old covenant, one should read Hebrews 8:7-13. He is supposed to be expounding upon Jeremiah's prophecy in chapter 31:31-34, but he is on an altogether different page than the prophet. The apostle is saying in Hebrews 8:13 that the old covenant is out-of-date, so to speak, has waxed old, and is ready to vanish away. Yet, as we have stated in a previous chapter, they have extracted 484 passages from the so-called "old covenant, or testament," to help create the so-called "new covenant, or testament." In that case, how could it then be ready to wax old and vanish away? Paul seems to be totally oblivious as to what is meant by the prophet in Jeremiah 31:31-34, and he has also used more references from the Hebrew Scriptures than any other biblical contributor. Yeshua taught obedience to God's Holy Law and to the teaching of the Prophets; Paul ushered in "the righteousness of God without the Law, which is by faith in Jesus Christ" (Rom. 3:21,22) Totally untrue!

What of the Ten Commandments?

It never ceases to amaze us when people continuously say, "We are no longer under the law, we are under grace." Everything in the universe is governed by some kind of law. There are the laws of gravity, of nature, and even of the jungle. The sun, moon, stars and planets, which were ordained by the Creator (Psalm 8), are all governed by laws: The sun rises in the east and sets in the west; the moon has four quarters per month, and the stars – although one differs from another – all function in their orbits. The tides of the thousands of natural bodies of water ebb and flow, according to the will of their Creator, and a few grains of corn produce several ears.

The Ten Commandments, as recorded in Exodus 20:1-17, were given by the Most High to Moses and the children of Israel, and Israel's mission is to teach them to the world, both by precept and example.

According to the teaching of the prophets of the Hebrew Scriptures, the Ten Commandments are ever-enduring and cannot be changed or annuled. They forbid idolatry and the profanation of the Creator's name; they command the hallowing of the weekly Seventh-day Sabbath, and the honoring of one's father and mother; they prohibit murder, adultery, stealing, bearing false witness against one's neighbor, and coveting anyone or anything which belongs to one's neighbor.

Those who say that the commandments are done away with and that we are now under grace, are really saying, in unawareness, that it is all right to dishonor parents, to murder, to commit adultery, and to steal, etc. "We are no longer under the law," say they, "but under grace."

Others say that it is impossible to keep the Ten Commandments. By making that declaration, they are saying that the Creator has commanded us to do something that we cannot do. The implication here is that He is unjust and unfair.

Do you know of anyone who would go before a judge in a court of law and say to him/her, 'Your honor, you cannot sentence me to jail for the crime I committed which was against the law, because I am not under the law, I am under grace?' Of course not. Neither do we think that is acceptable in the judgment of God.

Someone came along one or two hundred years into the Common Era (A.D.), after the Greek Scriptures had been compiled and canonized, and named the Hebrew Scriptures *the Old Testament,* strongly implying that it was no longer binding or valid. By so doing, it paved the way for the introduction of the Greek Scriptures as *the New Testament.* Christianity is greatly dependent upon what was established by the Most High through Moses and the prophets. The Pope of Rome himself has stated: "Christianity came out of Judaism." He should know; after all, Catholicism is the mother of all Christendom.

When you get right down to it, brothers and sisters, of all ten of the commandments, there is really only one with which the world has a problem, and that is God's Holy Sabbath, commonly called Saturday. Deep within people's heart of hearts they believe that they should abide by all the other commandments, but they become awfully upset when you mention the Holy Sabbath Day. Even though Yeshua (Jesus, their proclaimed Lord and Saviour) and Paul (the one whom most Christians are really following) observed it, the Sabbath seems to interfere with people's schedule. We have heard just about all the arguments as to why the Sabbath is not necessary. Here are a few of them: "It's the Jewish Sabbath"; "Any day can be your Sabbath, as long as you take one day a week"; "Nobody knows what day is the Sabbath; the calendar has been changed"; "We keep Sunday, because Jesus rose from the dead on Sunday"; and, of course, there's that old standby, "The Sabbath is the old Mosaic Law."

None of the above is true; let us prove it in a word:

The Sabbath is not 'Jewish'; Exodus 20:10 says that "it

is the Sabbath of the LORD thy God," and was established, blessed and hallowed long before there was a Jew on earth. If the Sabbath is Jewish, then "thou shalt not murder," "thou shalt not commit adultery," and "thou shalt not steal" would also have to be 'Jewish,' for they are all part of the same law – the Ten Commandments. ▪ Yes, any day can be your Sabbath, but the Creator said that "the seventh day is His Sabbath." Saturday is the seventh day of the week; look on any calendar throughout the world. ▪ It is said that "the calendar has been changed; we don't know when the Sabbath is." The sequence of days of the week has not changed. There are, and there have always been, seven days to the week universally; therefore, the Sabbath is still intact. ▪ Yeshua rose from the dead on Sunday? What does that have to do with God's Holy Sabbath? Absolutely nothing! Those who so-called 'keep Sunday' are doing so by command of the Roman Catholic Church (321 A.D.) and Emperor Constantine (325 A.D.), who made it punishable by death anyone found observing the holy Sabbath. Millions were slaughtered. ▪ And finally, the Sabbath is not the old Mosaic Law, but is part of the Holy Law of Almighty God.

Abundant blessings are promised in the Scriptures from the Most High to those who keep holy the Sabbath Day.

The Hebrew Scriptures' canon closes with the Book of Malachi, ending with chapter 4. More than 1000 years after the death of Moses the Almighty and Most High God in Malachi 4:4 commands:

> *"Remember ye the law of Moses My servant, which I command-ed unto him in Horeb* [Sinai] *for all Israel."*

The passage says, "Remember ye the 'law of Moses' . . ." It was not really Moses' law but the Creator's, inasmuch as He said, "which I commanded unto him in Horeb." The Eternal One gave the Law to Moses, Moses gave it to Israel, and Israel's mission is to give it to the world. For the LORD God has declared in Isaiah 49:6 (last part):

"I will also give thee [Israel] *for a light to the Gentiles, that thou mayest be My salvation unto the end of the earth."*

The world is groping in spiritual darkness today because it has divorced itself from the commandments of God. Truly, they are the Ten Commandments of Love – Love of God and Love of Neighbor – and is the only solution to world peace. In Deuteronomy 6:5, the Creator commands:

"And thou shalt love the LORD thy God with all thine heart, and with all thy soul, and with all thy might."

And in Leviticus 19:18 the Most High further commands:

". . . Thou shalt love thy neighbor as thyself."

We dare say that there is not a Christian, a Muslim, an Israelite, or a Jew on the planet who does not believe that we should live according to the above commands. A Greek Scripture (NT) passage reads (I John 5:3):

"For this is the love of God, that we keep His commandments: and His commandments are not grievous."

In closing this chapter, we invite you to read and internalize – several times if necessary – Exodus chapter 20:1-17, if you have not already, and see how beautiful and how perfect is this document authored by the King of the universe. The chapter opens (with verses 2 and 3 as the first commandment): *[1] "And God spoke all these words, saying: [2] 'I am the LORD thy God, who brought thee out of the land of Egypt, out of the house of bondage. [3] Thou shalt have no other gods before Me.'"* One not an adherent of the Israelite way may respond: "I've never been under Egyptian bondage; how could this apply to me?" We reply: Think of the many times when you were in distress and cried out unto the Almighty One, and He came to your rescue, took your feet out of the 'miry clay,' established your going, and put a new song in your mouth. Those were the times when you were in bondage." Honor your Great Creator by striving to keep His commandments.

CHAPTER 10

Crucifixion, Resurrection, Ascension, Alive Forever?

OF ALL THAT WE HAVE EVER WRITTEN – and probably of all that we will ever write – this topic will undoubtedly be the most controversial.

The Crucifixion

In this segment we will discuss the site of Yeshua's execution, reported to be *Calvary* (also known as *Golgotha*), as well as some of the events leading up to his death, and the reasons for Rome's decision to crucify him. Following this, we will present our own astounding assessment from the standpoint of logic and from truths that for centuries have been hidden – truths outside of the Greek Scriptures' report. We write; You the Reader draw your own conclusions.

How odd, but true, that with the mere mention of the words *crucify* and *crucifixion,* the minds of hundreds of millions the world over automatically go only to the death of Yeshua on the cross, not taking into account that thousands before Yeshua had been crucified by the Romans over the centuries. It is said that two thieves met their fate at the same time in the same way as Yeshua, but *crucifixion* and *crucify* seldom, if ever, bring their fates to mind.

Compare the following sources and see if they agree or differ:

FROM SMITH'S BIBLE DICTIONARY OF ca. 1863 –

Calvary (*a bare skull*). GOLGOTHA. *Place of the crucifixion of Jesus. Wm. C. Prime this year* [note that this was in the year

104

<u>1871:</u> author] *found a wall in Jerusalem which <u>he thinks</u> is the long-lost second wall of Josephus, running south of the so-called Church of the Holy Sepulchre, and <u>so far</u> proves the claim that <u>the true site of Calvary and the sepulchre are known and in that church.</u>*

Golgotha, from Smith's Bible Dictionary: (*a skull*), (Matt. 27:33). *Where Jesus was crucified, outside Jerusalem. The city at that time had a wall about Zion and another about Acra. Beyond these, to the north, the suburbs were enclosed by another wall by Agrippa. This seems to leave no place for the site of the crucifixion on that side, and <u>therefore the claim is denied of the present Church of the Holy Sepulchre is as being built over the tomb of Jesus.</u>*

FROM THE CYCLOPEDIC-DICTIONARY (1985) by Philip Schaff, D.D., LL.D., professor of Church History, Union Theological Seminary, New York:

Calvary/Golgotha (*skull*), *an elevation in the shape of a skull. The word* **Calvary** *used in the original means a skull, and was properly rendered by the Latin translators* **Calvarium.** *The translation of the English Version retained the Latin word, giving it an English termination . . . The place where Christ was crucified, near Jerusalem, but outside its walls. John 19:20. <u>The exact location of Calvary is unknown.</u>*

We see from the three accounts above that the location of Calvary/Golgotha is uncertain.

Why Was Yeshua Crucified?

About *65 years before the dawn of the Common Era (the C.E./A.D. time period) the Romans conquered the Greeks and the rest of the known world, including Jerusalem, the capital city of Judæa and the holy city of the Israelites. Both the proselytizer Yochanan (John) and Yeshua (Jesus) were born right in the midst of Roman rule. There was much resentment between Rome and the Israelites because Rome had invaded and completely taken over their land. (*See footnote, p. 113.)

After Yochanan had been beheaded for speaking out against the status quo of the Roman government and proclaiming that it was unlawful for Herod to have his brother Philip's wife, right on the heels of Yochanan came Yeshua, drawing great crowds and speaking out against the Gentiles and others among the ungodly.

The Sanhedrin, composed of Romans, Greeks and Edomite Jews, was the ruling court of the day. The Roman authorities arrested Yeshua on charges of blasphemy and sedition. The Sanhedrin tried him and found him guilty as charged.

The Documentation. A creditable Atlas entitled FORTY CENTURIES: FROM THE PHAROAHS TO ALFRED THE GREAT, published by The Britannica Society, states: *"It is our intent to give a fresh look at the Jesus of history, and tell, among other things, how the Romans were totally responsible for his crucifixion, and not the Jews, as the N.T. account depicts."*

The article continues: *"For the Romans alive about A.D. 30, the life and death of Jesus was of no significance whatsoever. In the context of Roman history, Jesus was just another rebellious trouble-maker. After the revolt of Spartacus thousands of slaves had been crucified in the same way as Jesus. His death was merely one more item in the list of repressions that Rome found necessary to carry out in order to consolidate her power.* **The early Christian authors were obviously concerned with transferring the responsibility for the crucifixion of Jesus from the Romans to the Jews."**

BUT WHAT SAY WE ON THE SUBJECT OF THE CRUCIFIXION, RESURRECTION & ASCENSION?

We believe that Yeshua was crucified. However, there are other schools of thought on the subject, one of which says that Yeshua had a twin brother, and that it was he whom the Romans executed. On that opinion we are mute.

Do we believe all of what has been recorded in the Greek Scriptures (NT) on the subject? No, we do not, as there have been too many lies, discrepancies and inconsistencies in other aspects of Yeshua's life as carried in the Gospels, which hinder us from "running with the herd." A few of the reasons follow:

The immaculate conception and virgin birth of Yeshua are untrue; for if he did not have a human father, how could he have been descended from David? He would have to have been a descendant of the Holy Ghost, since Matthew and Luke state that the child in Miriam's (Mary's) womb was of the Holy Ghost. Caucasian Christianity has changed him from a Black Hebrew Israelite to the White founder of Christianity. They have prevaricated concerning his messiahship, his being the only begotten son of God, and as the saviour of the world through his death on the cross, dying for the sins of the trillions of people who have already lived and died, the more than six billion now alive, and the trillions yet unborn. (All of the above are covered in-depth in our book, *A NON-CHRISTIAN'S RESPONSE TO CHRISTIANITY*.)

If the powers that were have lied about all of the above and more, why do you think that they will tell the whole truth about the Crucifixion, the Resurrection, and the Ascension?

BUCKLE UP! YESHUA SURVIVED THE CROSS!

Yes, Yeshua was crucified, **but he did not <u>die</u> on the cross – he survived the crucifixion, lapsing into a state of unconsciousness. The sponge filled with vinegar administered to Yeshua, as** recorded in Matt. 27:48, Mk. 15:36, Lu. 23:36, and Jn. 19:29-30, was really a type of chloroform or drug to send him into a stupor, as planned. Luke says that a soldier 'offered' him the vinegar. The other three Gospel writers report that witnesses of the crucifixion gave him the sponge-filled vinegar, and he drank it. **The Roman soldiers <u>thought</u> that he was dead.**

Joseph of Arimathæa, a rich man, begged his body – also as planned – and laid him in his tomb after using his influence and wealth to have his wounds treated and bound. Yeshua had learned the secrets of survival under the most severe conditions during his absence for those 18 years – from age 12 to age 30, on which the Bible is completely silent. (Where was he during those 18 years? In India and Egypt, studying.) After a portion of three days (Friday night, Saturday, and early Sunday morning) he recovered and re-appeared.

Some Others Who Survived Capital Punishment

There is a non-biblical story in the annals of Hebrew literature that tells how Abram of Ur, Babylonia, smashed into a thousand smitherines his father's many lesser idols and placed the hammer into the hand of the great idol. His father, upon returning from a journey, demanded of Abram an explanation. Abram replied, "The idols began fighting, and the great idol smashed the smaller ones." Father Terah in disbelief hailed Abram before Nimrod, ruler of Babylon, **and he had Abram cast into a fiery furnace. An angel of God rescued him from the devouring flames.** (This has been an abbreviated version of the story.) Genesis chapter 12 records "the call of Abraham" by the Most High God, saying, *"Get thee out of thy country, and from thy kindred, and from thy father's house, unto a land that I will shew thee."* .

Biblical survivors include: **Daniel, miraculously delivered from the lions' den. ■ the three Hebrew children – Hananiah, Azariah, and Mishael** (Shadrach, Meshach, and Abed-nego) – **from a fiery furnace ■ Jonah, from the belly of a great fish ■** and **Jeremiah, from a dungeon of miry clay** (quicksand), all through the power of Almighty God. **So why could not Yeshua have survived the crucifixion through the power of the Divine hand?**

"THE MIRACLE IN TRIPLICATE"

An Englishman who cheated the gallows, some claim by Divine intervention, was John Lee.

"The miracle in triplicate" occurred in Exeter, England, on February 23, 1885, when John Lee mounted the scaffold to be executed for the murder of Emma Keyse, one time maid-of-honor to Queen Victoria. The trapdoor under the scaffold failed to open. Three times John Lee mounted the scaffold. Three times the trapdoor did not function. After the third attempt, Lee was returned to the condemned cell, and his death sentence commuted to life imprisonment. John Lee served 22 years in prison. After his release from prison he emigrated to the U.S., where he married and never re-offended. He died in 1933.

The Gospels report that there were five wounds inflicted upon Yeshua during the crucifixion: two in his hands, two in his feet, and one in his side. Although we do not know the extent of his injuries, they must have ranged from serious to critical for him to have cried out in agony with a loud voice, *"Eli, Eli, lä'-mä să-băch'-thă-nī?"* that is to say, *"My God, my God, why hast Thou forsaken me?"*

There is an untold number of true stories wherein people have been seriously and even critically injured in wars, plane crashes, automobile and hazardous industrial accidents, who have recovered through proper medical care. Some of them have even endured their injuries for several days before being discovered and rescued, and against all odds have miraculously escaped the grasp of death. Again we ask: Why could not Yeshua?

Both the Hebrew Scriptures and the Greek Scriptures cite instances of people being raised from the dead. Those prophets who readily come to mind that demonstrated this power were Elijah, Elisha and Yeshua. But in every case, those resurrected still died again at a later time, as in the epics of the widow woman's son (with Elijah as the prophet); the Shunammite woman's son (with Elisha as the prophet), and Lazarus (with Yeshua as the prophet). But Christianity has Yeshua hanging on a cross for three hours and then dying, being buried in a tomb for a portion of three days, being resurrected from the dead, ascending into heaven, sitting on the right hand of God, and alive for evermore. There are absolutely no prophecies in the Hebrew Scriptures to support any of the above or any of the other claims which Christianity purports to have taken place in the life of Yeshua.

Did Yeshua Ascend to Heaven?

In a word: <u>No!</u> And the first chapter of Acts of the Apostles holds the main key to our conclusion. It should be known that Luke, a Caucasian Greek, who never saw Yeshua or any of his disciples, is the author of the book of Acts. Chapter 1, verse 3 tells how Yeshua showed himself alive to his apostles (formerly called disciples) for forty days after his resurrection. Verses 6 and 7 state:

> [6]*"When they* [Yeshua and the apostles] *therefore had come together, they asked of him, saying, 'Lord, wilt thou at this time restore again the kingdom to Israel?'* [7]*And he said unto them, 'It is not for you to know the times or the seasons, which the Father hath put in His own power.'"*

We see in verse 6 that when they asked Yeshua would he at this time restore again the kingdom to Israel, that he did not give them a direct 'yes' or 'no' answer, but told them that the Father [God] has put that time or season in His own power. Since Yeshua had not restored the kingdom to Israel prior to his crucifixion, as the Hebrew Scriptures have foretold that the Messiah will do, the apostles believed that whereas he had shown his power in rising from the dead, would shortly ascend to heaven and live for ever, surely before departing he would now fulfill the Messianic prophecies. John the Baptist had also inquired of Yeshua (in Matthew 11:3), "Art thou he that should come [or, 'are you the Messiah?'], or do we look for another?" In both instances – in Matthew and in Acts – he did not give a straightforward answer, but rather somewhat evaded the questions. (Read Matt. 11:1-4.) Even up to Yeshua's very last day on this earth, according to Acts, the apostles were still anxious about when the Messiah would fulfill the long-awaited promises. Only the Messiah, who is yet to come, is destined to restore the kingdom to Israel, abolish wickedness and usher in the everlasting state of peace.

Acts 1:9-11 are very important if we are to answer the question, **"Did Jesus Ascend to Heaven"**(?):

> [9]*"And when he had spoken these things, while they beheld, <u>he was taken up; and a cloud received him out of their sight.</u> [10]And while they looked stedfastly toward heaven as he went up, behold, two men stood by them in white apparel; [11]Which also said, Ye men of Galilee, why stand ye gazing up into heaven? This same Jesus, which is taken up from you into heaven, shall so come in like manner as ye have seen him go into heaven."*

According to the verses above, no one actually saw Yeshua "ascend into heaven" -- neither the apostles nor the two men in white. All they beheld was his *"being taken up and a cloud receiving him out of their sight."* From that time till now billions have assumed that Yeshua is in heaven, sitting at the right hand of God, and is alive for ever. This is the result when there is a misinterpretation of what has been written. An airplane becomes airborne and ascends into the clouds, yet we never say that the airplane is in heaven. But when Yeshua is taken up and a cloud receives him out of sight, Christianity says that he went to heaven. We speak of extra tall buildings as "skyscrapers," but do they actually scrape the sky? No; the term "skyscraper" is a figure of speech. Where the eagles fly is a "heaven"; the mountain peak is a "heaven," and the same is true of the sun, moon, stars, planets, and other constellations, seen and unseen, known and unknown.

The scriptures tell of Enoch, Moses, Elijah and Yeshua experiencing mysterious disappearances. II Kings 2:11 relates how that the prophet Elijah "went up by a whirlwind into heaven." This is not to say that the body of Elijah is in the abode of the Creator, who is SPIRIT, and has declared that *"I fill both heaven and earth"* (Jer. 23:23,24). This DIVINE INTELLIGENCE is so Almighty that no human or group of humans has ever or will ever comprehend the full Manifestation of ITS DIVINE ESSENCE. If all six billion present-day earthlings would worship Him in one accord at the same time, in the thousands of various languages and dialects, it would still be insufficient. King Solomon in his prayer of Temple dedication (I Kings 8:27) extolled the greatness of the Most High thusly::

"But will God indeed dwell on the earth? Behold, <u>the heaven and heaven of heavens cannot contain Thee; how much less this house that I have builded?"</u>

<u>Anthropomorphism</u> is defined as, *"representation or conception of God, or of a god, with human attributes; also, ascription of human characteristics to things not human."* Not only is the Bible crammed with figures of speech, but it also possesses an abundance of anthropomorphism, i.e., speaking of the Almighty Divine Being in human terms. The Scriptures have ascribed to the Creator the gender of *male,* hence the use of *Him* and *His* hundreds of times. Man in Scripture has given the Creator *eyes, ears, hands, feet, a nose,* and even *feathers* and *wings,* as in Psalm 91:4. All these comparisons are made, nonetheless, to help convey a better understanding of that which is not fully known – the Creator – to that which is known – Man.

A Cloud Received Yeshua, Then What?

Let us review Acts 1:10-11 again, and hear exactly what is being said here:

[10]*"And while they looked stedfastly <u>toward heaven</u> as he went up, behold, two men stood by them in white apparel;* [11]*Which also said, Ye men of Galilee, why stand ye gazing up into heaven? This same Jesus, which is taken up from you into heaven, shall so come in like manner as ye have seen him go into heaven."*

When one is outdoors without obstruction, and looks up, he is looking <u>"toward heaven."</u> The two men who stood in white apparel beside the apparently disappointed apostles spoke comfortably and appeasingly to them with words of encouragement that Yeshua would come again. The verse says nothing of them being sent by the Most High, or of their declaration being a revelation from Him. Neither were they prophets of God, but simply <u>"men</u> in white apparel." It is not surprising that the Christians' holy book – the Greek Scriptures – would lend unwavering support to the ascension of Yeshua, since it is rigorously linked to their belief in his second coming. **We say emphatically that Yeshua (Jesus) is not in heaven sitting at the right hand of the Great I AM, for the Great I AM, which is SPIRIT, literally has no "right hand." And since there is no prophecy or promise in either the Hebrew Scriptures or the Greek Scriptures from the Almighty God Itself/"Himself" which supports one of Christianity's foremost beliefs, *"the Second Coming of Christ,"* we refuse to believe that Yeshua ben Yosef (whom the Greeks named Jesus) is coming to earth again.**

THERE IS EVIDENCE FROM THE ANCIENT COUNTRY OF INDIA WHICH REVEALS THAT AFT-ER YESHUA's (JESUS') ASCENT, HE MOVED TO INDIA NEAR THE HIMALAYA MOUNTAINS RE-GION, WHERE HE LIVED TO BE 75 YEARS OLD.

According to the Roman Calendar and the present Christian record, Yeshua's crucifixion took place on Friday, April 13, A.D. 33. The early Sunday morning resurrection (Matt. 28:1) brings us to April 15. Acts 1:3 reveals that Yeshua was seen of his apostles [for] forty days after his passion. Forty days after April 15 is May 25, A.D. 33, which is the approximate date of his ascension. May 25, 2033, therefore, will mark 2,000 years since "a cloud received him [Yeshua] out of their sight" (Acts 1:9).

The conclusion of the whole matter on the subjects at hand -- the Cricifixion, the Resurrection, and the Ascension – is that all these stories can be traced back many centuries before to Egyptian and Babylonian mythology; to the sixth century Persian Mithraic Cult, and to Greek and Roman mythology. (See our book entitled *WHAT WILL IT TAKE TO WAKE US UP?* -- the chapter, *"Mithraism: Forerunner of Christianity."*)

"The Half Has Not Been Told!"

*Correction on page 105, near bottom: In our First Printing we stated that the Romans conquered the Greeks ca. 200 B.C.E. Actually, it was ca. 65 B.C.E.

CHAPTER 11

O! To Be Black!

I HAVE SEEN *The Malcolm X Story* now a total of three times – once in the movies and twice on television. For those of you who also saw it, I am sure you remember the scene where the brother who was already encarcerated before Malcolm arrived, was telling him about the Honorable Elijah Muhammad. During that episode, you recall how the brother opened the dictionary and showed Malcolm (played by Denzell Washington) the definition of the word **black.** Every definition was all negative, from beginning to end.

In all of my 76+ years I had never, never looked up the word *black* in the dictionary for myself, as dictionary-savvy and as word-conscious as I thought I was. Even when 'the brother' showed Malcolm the 'European' definition of *black,* it still didn't register; for I thought while watching the story, "I wonder is that really the definition of the word *black,* or is that something that the writers, producers and directors of the movie are making up in order to enhance the picture? Or that 'the brother' must be reading from an antiquated version of a dictionary, for this could not possibly be what the White race thinks of *Blacks* and *blackness* in this day and time."

So while I was contemplating what to write as the last chapter of this book, that part of the *Malcolm X Story* where 'the brother' was enlightening Malcolm came forcibly to mind. On Saturday night, November 25, 2006, at 8:45 p.m., I reached for my Webster's Collegiate Dictionary to check out the definition of the word **black** for the very first time in my life. And there it was, just as 'the brother' in the film had said:

> <u>black</u> 1. **Destitute of light, or incapable of reflecting it; devoid of color or so dark as to have no distinguishable color; -- opposed to** *white*. **2. Enveloped in darkness; devoid of light; hence, utterly dismal or gloomy; as, the future looked** *black*. **3. Having dark skin, hair, and eyes; specif., pertaining or belonging to a race characterized by dark pigmentation, including Negroes, Negritos, and Australian natives. 4. Soiled with dirt; foul. 5. Wearing black garments; as, the** *black* **knight. 6. Sullen; hostile; foreboding; as,** *black* **looks. 7. <u>Foully or outrageously wicked;</u> as,** *black* **cruelty 8. Indicating disgrace or dishonor, or culpability; as, a** *black* **mark. 9. Involving baneful or forbidden practices; as,** *black* **magic. 10.** *U.S.* **Inveterate; dyed-in-the-wool; as, a** *black* **Republican. 11. Sold, distributed, or charged in violation of official quotas, ceiling prices, priorities, or ration restrictions, or conducted for such sale or distribution; as,** *black* **rent;** *black* **market. --** *n.* **1. The darkest color, ideally that represented by total absence of light or resulting from total absorption of all light rays. 2. Something black or dark-colored. 3. A Negro, Negrito, or Australian native; loosely, one of a dark-skinned race or one having some Negro blood.**

So as 'the brother' in the movie did, so did I – I went to the dictionary and looked up the word **white** for the very first time in my life. And there it was, just as 'the brother' had said:

> <u>white</u> 1. **Of the color of pure snow; reflecting to the eye all the rays of the spectrum combined; -- the opposite of** *black* **or** *dark*. **2. Hence, light or relatively light in color; as,** *white* **wine;** *white hair*; **lips** *white* **with fear; the snow made it a** *white* **Christmas. 3. Free from spot or blemish; hence, in-**

nocent; pure. 4. Without evil in intent; relatively harmless; as, a *white* lie; *white* magic. 5. *Now Rare.* Fortunate; auspicious. 6. a, Having a light-colored skin; Caucasian; as, a *white* man. b. Composed of or controlled by the *white* race; as, the policy of a *white* Australia. c. *Orig. Slang, U.S.* Honest; square-dealing; honorable.

You haven't seen or heard anything yet! I went to my computer, typed the word *black,* clicked on "Tools" on the top bar, and then clicked on "Thesaurus." As you know, the synonyms for a word in the thesaurus appear in alphabetical order. Using the mouse, the synonyms went from *a* to *w*. What do you think the very first synonym for *black* is in the thesaurus? You guessed it right: **"abominable"**.

The thesaurus carries 188 synonyms for *black;* of the entire list there are only three words that are not utterly negative. I took the time to painstakingly copy by hand every synonym from the computer's thesaurus for the word *black.* The list is as follows:

abominable	charcoal	dour	glum
absolute	clouded	downright	gook
angry	coal	dreary	grave
apocalyptic	complete*	dusky	gray
arrant	crow	ebony	grievous
asperse	damnable	embargo	grim
awful	dark	evil	grubby
bad	darkness	execrable	grum
baleful	deadly	fatal	hateful
baneful	deathly	felonious	heinous
base	defame	filthy	hellish
blacken	dejected	flagitious	ill
blacklist	depressing	foreboding	ill-fated
blameworthy	destructive	foul	ill-starred
bleak	diabolical	frowning	improper
boy	dire	funebrial	impure
brunet	disastrous	funereal	inaccurate
calamitous	disgraceful	furious	inauspicious
cataclysmic	dismal	gloomy	inexpedient
catastrophic	doomful	glowering	infamous

inferior
infernal
iniquitous
ink
inky
insidious
interdict
invalid
jet
jetty
knavish
libel
low
lowering
malevolent
malicious
malignant
melancholy
menacing
midnight
monstrous
moody
mopey
moping
morose
mourning
nasty
naughty
nefarious
night
obscure
obscured
ominous
oppressive
out-and-out
outrageously
outright
peccant
perfect*
perfidious
pitch
pitchy
portentous
positive*
rank
raven
rayless

regular
reprehensible
reprobate
resentful
ruinous
sable
saturnine
scandalous
scurry
shameful
sinful
sinister
slander
slate
sloe
slur
smear
smoke
smut
solemn
somber
soot
sooty
spade
squalid
starless
sullen
sunless
surly
swarthy
tar
tarry (tar-ry)
tanebrous
threatening
tragic
treacherous
triste
unclean
unconscionable
unfavorable
unforgivable
unfortunate
unhealthy
unilluminated
unkind
unlit
unlucky

unpardonable
unpleasant
unprincipled
unpromising
unpropitious
unscrupulous
unskillful
unspeakable
untoward
unworthy
vicious
vile
vilify
villainous
wearisome
weary
wicked
wrathful
wrong

*Denotes positive synonym. (Just 3 in all.)

There you have it, brothers and sisters – 185 reasons to hate yourself if you are of African ancestry and <u>don't know your history</u>.

There are 157 synonyms in the computer's thesaurus for the word *white*. Time and space will not allow me to publish the entire list, but I will present some examples of what it comprises. These are just 23 of the many, many positives:

white: advanced / auspicious / bright / clean / fairness / fortunate / immaculate / impeccable / innocent / kosher / nonpolluted / pearl / pure / pure-hearted / royalist / spotless / unadulterated / unblemished / undefiled / unpolluted / unspotted / venerable / virtuous.

Some of the negatives, only 14 in all, include:

white: barren / blank / blimp / bloodless / characterless / dead / devoid / diehard / dim / empty / fallow / ghastly / maggot / null & void.

Percentage-wise, the **black list** contains 13 times more derogatory and degrading words than the **white** negative list. A young unknowledgeable black person reading the list which has been applied to us would certainly have his self-esteem shattered and would feel, *"What's the use of my even trying to make something of myself, if all of those descriptions apply to me? I might as well become a criminal, if that listing describes who and what I really am."*

Thank God Almighty, I can look at all 185 words of that wicked, abominable catalog of putridity and cry tears of joy, as I am doing right now, and rejoice within my very soul that **"I am somebody,"** and have been taught so from age five till now. As a **black** race of people, we are descended from kings, queens, princes and princesses. What makes us the strongest people in the world is the fact that we have endured and survived 348 years of institutionalized slavery in the western hemisphere. Any people who endures what our fore-parents, and we ourselves, have endured for that length of time and beyond, can go through anything. Hold your head high, **black men and black women,** and don't allow that list of derogatives cause you to minimize your self-esteem. **Black is Beautiful!** And the proof is forthcoming.

The list has dehumanized all Black people from the Pharoahs to the Egyptian boy king Tutankhamun to Hannibal. It has villified all the great Black people of the 19th and 20th centuries, such as Booker T. Washington, Marcus Garvey, Phyllis Wheatley, Harriet Tubman, Alice Walker, Dr. George Washington Carver, William Saunders Crowdy, and W. E. B. Dubois. (The list is inexhaustible.) Those who have compiled and published the dictionaries and thesauruses carrying such atrocious descriptions of the Black race have done so with the intent to enslave us emotionally, mentally and spiritually. There are thousands of us who have enough knowledge of self who are going to strive to deliver our people who are willing from mental and spiritual bondage, even if it is done a few at a time. We are going to *'lift as we climb.'* Here is how and where you can begin:

Make copies from this book of the dictionary definitions and the computer's thesaurus synonyms on the word **black**, and distribute them to every Black person with whom you come into contact. Tell them to check the dictionary and computer thesaurus for themselves, in the event they don't believe the hand-out. Encourage them to trust in the Almighty God, to have faith in themselves, and to go to school and obtain a marketable skill. We can start right here to turn our race around and place them on the road to self-help and recovery.

The definitions from the Webster's Collegiate Dictionary and the synonyms from the computer's thesaurus have served at least one good purpose: They have confirmed what the White race, for the most part, thinks of us as members of the Black race. Is there any wonder that Whites feel so much more superior to Blacks, after they read the accounts from such supposedly authentic sources?

LET US GO TO THE SCRIPTURES

There are at least three instances in the Hebrew Scriptures where the disobedient and rebellious caused the anger of the Most High to be kindled against them, and the result was that they were stricken with leprosy and were turned *white*. Miriam, the sister of Moses, was such a victim; she and Aaron spoke against Moses because he had married a Black Ethiopian woman. (Read Numbers 12:1-13.)

Back in the mid-1980s I presented a lecture at Kingsborough College in Brooklyn, NY, from the topic, *Were the Original Jews Black?* Strangely enough, it was the chairman of the History Department, Mr. Kaplan, who asked me repeatedly to consider doing the lecture, and it was he also who even chose the topic and had the posters which the college had printed placed all over the campus. Many Jewish faculty members were present as I spoke of Moses and all the Hebrew prophets, priests and kings of biblical times as Black men.

During the question and answer period several faculty members and students asked questions. I remember till this day one question in particular which was asked by a Jewish professor. He stated, *"You said in your presentation that Moses was Black. If he was indeed Black, why did his brother and sister speak against him for marrying a Black woman?"* The answer came very easy: "Yes, Moses was Black, and the Cushite (Ethiopian) woman he married was also Black. Aaron and Miriam did not speak against Moses because he had married out of his race, but because she wasn't an Israelite, as the law of Israel required. Not only was Moses Black, but so were all the other biblical prophets from Abraham through Malachi, and all the Israelites of biblical times." Upon hearing the answer the professor took his seat without any opposing comments. I didn't tell the audience, but Yeshua (Jesus) and all his disciples were also Black; not one White disciple did he have.

THE ANCIENT HAMITES' CONTRIBUTIONS

The ancient Egyptians, Ethiopians, Babylonians, and Assyrians were all Hamitic in origin, and established the greatest civilizations ever. You can read about them on page 16 in my book *"The Deceiving of the Black Race."*

Let us take a brief look at the man Ham, one of the sons of Noah. He and his descendants settled in Africa, and sent many branches into Asia (the entire Canaanite family of nations; Gen. 10). Psa. 78:51, 105:23, and 106:22 mention Egypt as the "land of Ham." In Zephaniah 3:10 the Most High God calls the Ethiopians "My suppliants" and "the daughters of My dispersed," saying:

"From beyond the rivers of Ethiopia My suppliants, even the daughters of My dispersed, shall bring Mine offering."

A *suppliant* is "one who makes supplication; a petitioner. Expressive of supplication."

Ethiopia, Egypt, and Libya – all African countries – are mentioned in scripture hundreds of times. We have yet to see France, Germany, Switzerland, etc., in the Holy Book. The ancient Israelites were even descended from the Hamitic Canaanites and Babylonians. This statement will probably cause quite a stir, but we can prove it.

"The descendants of Ham – Egypt and Babylon -- led the way as pioneers in art, literature and science. Mankind at the present day lies under infinite obligations to the genius and industry of those early ages, more especially for alphabetic writing, weaving, cloth, architecture, astronomy, plastic, art, sculpture, navigation and agriculture. The art of painting is also represented, and music indirectly, by drawings of instruments." (From Smith's Bible Dictionary of 1863.)

So when the dictionary defines **black** as *indicating disgrace or dishonor, foul, outragously wicked,* among many other unfounded descriptions, just know that it is telling a most damnedable lie, when you consider the above contributions that the ancient Black nations have made to civilization.

And when the thesaurus equates **black** with *abominable, blameworthy, disgraceful, filthy, hellish* (and much more), just know that you come from a wise and ancient people who set in motion thousands of years ago all that the White race is capitalizing on today.

We are fully aware that the dictionary and thesaurus in their tirades are not targeting black animals or the blackness that exists in much of nature, such as the black night sky or the black pearl from the sea. The publications' focuses are on *Black people.*

Since we are a part of nature, if we are evil, wicked and abominable as Black people, then the thing from which we were formed – the dust of the ground and all the minerals that are in the earth – would also have to be wicked, evil and abominable.

Everything that exists came forth out of blackness. The Creator of the universe Himself "has said that He would dwell in thick darkness" (I Kings 8:12). Human beings are in the blackness of their mothers' wombs for nine months. All vegetation – edible and non-edible – has its roots in darkness under the ground. A photograph is taken, and is developed in the darkroom. Every thought that man thinks – good or evil – comes from the blackness of his mind. It is in the blackness and still of the night that the earth replenishes itself and that human beings while asleep become renewed. And on, and on, and on.

"Everything Black is Evil," They Say

If a 'black cat' crosses your path, it's bad luck. With cowboys, the good guys wear the white hats, the bad guys wear the black hats. There's "the black market" and the "black sheep" of the family. A person commits a crime, and it is said that "he has a 'dark' side to his character." When problems arise it is said that "things are looking very dark." A person who deals unscrupulously is said "to be a 'shady' character." If you're not liked, you are put on one's "black list," put in his "little back book," or you are "black-balled." Angel food cake is *white;* Devil food cake is **black.** The little Black girl has two dolls – one black and one white. She constantly hugs and kisses, and combs the white doll's hair. She spanks and scolds the black doll without cause. Before long you see the black doll leaning over in the corner of the room with an arm and a leg off, and its head twisted to the side. The little girl has been taught to hate **black** because of the images she has seen on TV and in life in general.

It seems that the only good thing about **black** is *Black Friday* – the Friday after Thanksgiving Day, when the merchants take advantage of the opportunity to move from operating in the "red" to moving into the *"black."*

During and since the days of slavery many whites referred to our people as "darkies." They even included it in some of their songs, such as, *I've Been Working On the Railroad," "Carry Me Back to Old Virginny," and "Way Down Upon the Swannie River."*

Be encouraged, brothers and sisters; **"everything that has a beginning has an ending!"** Slavery in the western hemisphere lasted for 348 years – from 1517 to 1865. We can't even imagine how many millions perished in the Middle Passage or how many millions were born and died during that 348-year period. What about all the heartache, rapes, lynchings, burnings, castrations, whippings and selling of family members that went on during those three-and-a-half centuries. Institutionalized slavery did finally end as a result of the North winning the Civil War. It wasn't Abraham Lincoln who freed the slaves, for history declares: "Lincoln did that which was right, but not because it was right. He signed the [so-called] Emancipation Proclamation to save the Union."

Thousands of Black soldiers fought in that War on the side of the Union Army, thus participating in their own freedom. It was none other than the power of the Almighty and Most High God which caused the Northern Union Army to be victorious. I tremble to think what would have been our plight had the Southern Confederate Army won!

Psalm 46:9-10 - *"He* [Almighty God] *maketh wars to cease unto the ends of the earth; He breaketh the bow, and cutteth the spear in sunder; He burneth the chariot in the fire. Be still, and know that I am God . . ."*

Considering how wicked the world has come to be – with racism, discrimination, prejudice and injustice on every side – if I had it to do all over again, and had a choice in the matter, in spite of it all I would still choose to be a **Black African Hebrew Israelite** – the seed of Abraham, God's friend for ever.

CHAPTER 12

The Hebrew Alphabet
& A Few Everyday Phrases

FOREWORD

I CONFESS, AND RIGHTLY SO, that I am by no means an authority on the Hebrew language. What little I have learned about it is attributed to my friend and brother, Rabbi Dahton Nasi (in the '70s), and my deceased beloved wife, Sister Naomi (2001-2003). It was not a daily or weekly involvement with me, but a "catch-as-catch-can", due to my pursuits in many other endeavors at the time. Both Rabbi Nasi and Sister Naomi were quite fluent in the language, as they organized Hebrew classes in a number of our associated congregations.

In my limited way, however, I will begin with the Hebrew *Alabet* (alphabet), how to pronounce each one, and then move on to a few everyday phrases.

~~~~~~~

There are 22 letters in the Hebrew alphabet. They are as follows:

Aleph - א (ÄH'-lĕf). Silent letter.

Bet - ב (Bĕt) or **Vet**. B as in Boy.

Gimmel - ג (Gĭm-MĔL). G as in Girl.

Dalet - ד (DÄ-lĕt). D as in Door.

Hey - ה (Hāy). H as in House.

125

Vav - ו (**Väv**). V as in Vine.

Zayin - ז (**ZÄ-yĭn**). Z as in Zebra.

Chet - ח (**Kĕt**). Ch as in BaCH.

Tet - ט (**Tĕt**). T as in Tall.

Yod - י (**Yōd**), (like code).Y as in Yes.

Kaf - כ ך פ (**Käf**). K as in Kitty;
CH as in BaCH.

Lamed - ל (**LÄ-mĕd**). L as in Look.

Mem - מ (Regular Mem) ם (Final Mem) (**Mĕm**).
M as in Mother.

Nun - נ (Regular Nun) ן (Final Nun) (**Noon**).
N as in Now.

Samech - ס (**Sä-MĔK**). S as in Sun.

Ayin - ע (**Ä-yin**). Silent letter.

Pey - פ ף (**Pāy**). P as in People.

Tsade - צ ץ (**T'sä-DĒ**). TS as in NuTS.

Qof - ק (**Koof**). K as in Kitty.

Resh - ר (**Rĕsh**). R as in Robin.

Shin - שׁ (**Shĭn**). SH as in Shape.

Sin - שׂ (**Sĭn**). S as in Sun.
If the dot is over the right prong, it's a Shin; over the left prong, it's a Sin.

Tav - ת (**Täv**). **T as in Tall.**

SOCIAL CONVERSATION

Hello   (lit. Peace)

שָׁלוֹם

shā-LŌM

Good morning

בֹּקֶר טוֹב

BŌ-kĕr töv

Good evening

עֶרֶב טוֹב

Ĕ-rĕv töv

Good night

לַיְלָה טוֹב

lāylāh TŌV

Goodbye   (lit. Peace)

שָׁלוֹם

sha-LOM

Excuse me

סְלִיחָה

s'lee-KHÄ

I'll see you later

לְהִתְרָאוֹת

l'-heet-ra-OT

How are things? (lit. What's being heard?)

מַה נִשְׁמָע

ma neesh-MA?

All right. (lit. In order)

הַכֹּל בְּסֵדֶר

ha-KOL B-SE-der

Thank you is: tō-DÄH

Yes is: cain

ABOUT THE AUTHOR

MOSES FARRAR was born in Richmond, Virginia, and is the youngest of eight children. At age seven he went to live in the Hampton Roads Virginia area, 90 miles southeast of Richmond. Shortly after his arrival there he was selected from among many others in his age group to be trained in printing, where he learned to set type by hand – one letter at a time. In the "old days" a beginner was called a "printer's devil." In 1941 his mother took him to Philadelphia to live. When old enough to enter high school he chose to attend Dobbins Vocational Technical High School, where he continued studies in printing. He has worked on the staff of several newspapers and book-making plants in Philadelphia and Virginia. In 1969 he opened his own printing business in Philadelphia, operating it for eight years.

Ordained an Elder of an international Israelite congregation in 1971 (of which he is virtually a life-long member), he has headed congregations in Atlantic City, NJ, Brooklyn, NY, New Haven, CT, Rochester, NY, and Philadelphia. After moving to Brooklyn in 1976, he again established his printing business there for 15 years.

He is considered by many to be among the leading biblicists, biblical historians and lecturers, having presented lectures and historical and spiritual seminars since 1980 at colleges and houses of worship of various religious persuasions. In 1991 Elder Farrar lectured from the stage of the world-famous Apollo Theater in Harlem, NY. The Author was chosen by the Chief Rabbi of his congregation to visit South Africa in 1991, 1992 and 1994, to assist in strengthening the spiritual work of our many associated congregations there. For 15 years he was a member of the religious panel for the training course, "Facilitating African-American Adoption," sponsored by the New York Chapter Association of Black Social Workers' Adoption Service.

Shortly after the death of his beloved wife, Naomi, in September 2004, he moved back to Philadelphia, where he now resides.

Farrar is listed in the 2000 and forward editions of *Who's Who Among African Americans.* His book titles include: *The Deceiving of the Black Race, A Non-Christian's Response To Christianity; The Hebrew Heritage of Black Africa* (co-author); *What Will It Take To Wake Us Up?; Lavinia My Mother, Naomi My Wife; Old Testament & New Testament: The Vast Differences; 40 Most FAQs (Frequently Asked Questions) To Hebrew Israelites – With Answers;* and *Yeshua/Jesus, Who Thought He Was Messiah.*

ORDER FORM FOR

BOOK No. 9:

"What Black Christians Should Know (But Don't) About Christianity!"

NO HOME IS COMPLETE WITHOUT THIS BOOK!

ALL BOOKS ARE $15.00 EACH

$3.00 S&H for 1 Book.

Add .95¢ for each add'l book mailed in 1 pkg.

Make check or m.o. payable to: "Moses Farrar"
Mail to: P.O. Box 3911, Philadelphia, PA 19146

Telephone: (215) 545-0548

- -

Enclosed is check/m.o. In the amount of $_____

for _____ copies of *"What Black Christians Should Know (But Don't) About Christianity,"* @ $15.00 each, plus S&H.

Name_____

Address_____

City_____ State_____ Zip_____

Telephone (   )_____. Date of Order_____

(See Order Form on Next Page)

Order Author's Books By Number

Send check/m.o. payable to: "MOSES FARRAR"
Mail to: P.O. BOX 3911 • PHILADELPHIA, PA 19146
Telephone: (215) 545-0548

Book No. 1: "The Deceiving of the Black Race"
112 Pages – $15.00. (Add $3.00 S&H; total $18.00)

Book No. 2:
"A Non-Christian's Response To Christianity"
152 Pages – $15.00. (Add $3.00 S&H; total $18.00)

Book No. 3: "The Hebrew Heritage of Black Africa"
128 pages – $15.00. (Add $3.00 S&H; total $18.00)

Book No. 4: "What Will It Take To Wake Us Up?"
76 Pages – $15.00. (Add $3.00 S&H; total $18.00)

Book No. 5:
"Lavinia My Mother, Naomi My Wife"
[In Memory] 90 Pp., w/Plx – $15.00. (Add $3.00 S&H; $18.00)

**Book No. 6: "The Hebrew Scriptures (O.T.) & The
Greek Scriptures (N.T.): The Vast Differences"**
132 Pages – $15.00. (Add $3.00 S&H; total $18.00)

Book No. 7:
**"40 Most FAQs (Frequently Asked Questions)
of Hebrew Israelites — with Answers"**
88 Pages – $15.00. (Add $3.00 S&H; total $18.00)

Book No. 8: "Rabbi Yeshua/Jesus Not The Messiah"
134 Pages – $15.00. (Add $3.00 S&H; total $18.00)

(Add.95c more S&H for each additional book mailed in one package)

Send me ____ copies of Book No. 1 @ $15.00 ea. Total: $_____
____ copies of Book No. 2 @ $15.00 ea. Total: $_____
____ copies of Book No. 3 @ $15.00 ea. Total: $_____
____ copies of Book No. 4 @ $15.00 ea. Total: $_____
____ copies of Book No. 5 @ $15.00 ea. Total: $_____
____ copies of Book No. 6 @ $15.00 ea. Total: $_____
____ copies of Book No. 7 @ $15.00 ea. Total: $_____
____ copies of Book # 8 @ $15.00 ea. Total: $_____
Enclosed is check/m.o. In the amount of $_____ for above books.
Name _____
Address _____
City _____ State _____ Zip _____
Telephone (_____) _____

- *NOTES* -